Manuscript Copyrig
Cover Art Copyrigh
Logo Copyright 202
Edited by Waylon Jo
Interior Design by W

No part of this book may be reproduced, stored in a retrieval system, or transmitted in any form or by any means, including mechanical, electric, photocopying, recording, or otherwise, without the prior written permission of the publisher or author

Roost
Hope Madden

Book 1: Hatchlings
1970

Easter Sunday

An old woman opens the front door of an untended bungalow. She wears her hair long, wiry, and loose. The sun is setting. Easter decorations bedeck the lawn next door. Graffiti on the wooden steps leading to her porch depict a broom and the words "Surrender Dorothy."

The woman looks heavenward, her eyes wide. She lets go a mirthless cackle, runs to her lawn, and yells, "Victory! Victory!"

Across the street at Peabody's gas station, customers stare.

A shadow—long, wide, winged—falls across her lawn. The old woman looks stricken. She shrieks. She screams, "No, no, no, no, no! I have been so good!"

She drops to her knees, then to her face on the lawn.

Not six blocks away, near a short, plump vase spilling with violets freshly picked from the Sisters of Mercy Hospital lawn, James and Maureen Murphy wearily grin at what many consider their late in life surprise: not one but two brand new Murphy girls they've named Joy and Hope.

It's an Easter miracle.

Book 2: Nestlings
1976

Easter Sunday

James and Maureen Murphy's green two-story at 93 Second Avenue sits on a small lot with no intentional landscaping. Two maples line the roadside out front. You can just make out the unkempt lilac bush around back at the kitchen window from the street. The lilacs won't properly purple until May, Maureen Murphy's favorite month. April, and all this waiting for the Lord's return, fill her with anxiety. Mrs. Murphy doesn't draw an easy breath until she's put April behind her.

The tidy front porch, concrete with a thin, black wrought iron rail, contains two white lawn chairs, a window that looks into Mr. Murphy's office, and a perpetually unlocked front door off to one side where two little girls make their way into the day.

Joy and Hope walk in the chilly sunshine of spring toward their neighbors' house. They are not especially pretty girls, both skinny with dull brown hair hanging to their waist. Hope wears glasses and stands a head taller than her sister, whose alert blue eyes scan the neighborhood. The two sing quietly as they make their way down the sidewalk past large, tidy old homes.

"Come be with me, come play with me, we'll go, you'll see," they sing. "Secret place, you and me, chickadee."

Today marks the girls' sixth birthday, which happens, as it did on the day they were born, to land on Easter Sunday.

Mass is concluded, lunch is finished, and Hope and Joy are allowed to walk down to the Cassidys' house to see if their friend, Brenda, can play.

They walk up the steps of a wide, open porch and ring the doorbell.

Mrs. Cassidy opens the door. She's sour-faced, wearing dark hair, streaked Bride-of-Frankenstein-style with white.

"On Easter Sunday?" She purses her lips. "Well, Brenda has to go check on the Gehrigs' house, so she can walk you back."

Mrs. Cassidy stares silently at the twins for a beat.

"Brenda!" she yells behind her without opening the screen door, and then to the twins: "People don't go visiting on Easter Sunday. Your parents should know better."

Brenda's lean with big eyes. She has the look of an insect – Brenda the Bug.

"Don't be gone all day," Mrs. Cassidy tells her, tucking her hair behind her ears. "Uncle Gary will be here soon."

Brenda starts to object.

"I don't want to hear it," Mrs. Cassidy shuts her down. "And make sure you don't get all dirty. Stay pretty and clean until your uncle can see you. He's missed you!"

Brenda joins the two on the front porch, and they all walk back toward Joy and Hope's house.

"It's our birthday," Hope says.

"It would stink to have a birthday on Easter," Brenda sympathizes.

"It's not always on Easter, though," Hope says. "Just sometimes."

"You can't have a party or anything because it's an important holiday, and everyone cares more about the Easter bunny and everything."

"We never have a birthday party," Hope says.

Brenda shakes her head, her curling-iron turned hair untucking from her ears as she does.

"My mom says you were born on Easter Sunday, and that was the same day an old witch died."

"She wasn't a witch," Joy corrects. "She was a misunderstood, poor old lady. That's what our mom says."

"My mom says we're better off without her scaring the kids," Brenda continues, "and that it was weird that she died when you were born. An ailment … alignment. Like it happened right at the same minute."

"Can't be the same minute," Hope says. "Joy's three minutes older. There's a bunch of minutes in there. Which minute was it?"

"Our mom says the Cassidys are very dramatic," Joy says. "She says it would be better for you to keep your eyes open and your mouths shut."

Taking offense, Brenda stops, mouth open, to stomp one foot.

Joy and Hope run ahead, singing.

"Secret place, you and me," they sing. "Chick, chick, chick, chick, chickadee."

Brenda waits a minute, then follows.

The three land on another wide, wooden porch, this one tan and badly in need of painting. Brenda produces the house key with an authoritative flourish.

"I'm supposed to feed their cat."

The Gehrigs live next door to Hope and Joy, who worry their parents will see them entering the empty home. Key or no, Mr. and Mrs. Murphy wouldn't want the girls inside the neighbors' house without adult supervision.

It's a big house with a second-floor apartment. Sometimes the Gehrigs take on tenants—usually single men. It's a small apartment.

The girls all know the house well. Holly Gehrig is younger, but they play with her sometimes.

Hank Gehrig drives a semi. When he's home, he keeps the cab of his truck parked in the backyard. Joy and Hope were in it once. He has a long poster of a naked woman hanging in the cramped sleeping space behind the driver's seat.

Honey is the youngest mom in the neighborhood. She wears cut-off shorts and lets a cigarette dangle from her lips when she hangs the laundry out back. Joy and Hope's older sisters say Honey entertains when Hank is away. Mrs. Murphy shushes them when they say it.

The girls shuffle through the shag carpet of the living room past the bedrooms and into the kitchen at the back of the house. Gladys, the Gehrigs' tabby, darts from behind a splitting leather couch and runs toward the children.

Joy and Hope stand quietly in the kitchen entranceway for a moment. Brenda opens the refrigerator and looks for a snack. Then she opens a can nested in a pack of cat food on the counter, dumping its contents into a bowl on the floor near the refrigerator.

The Murphy girls meander back into the living room. They thumb through albums, then pocket some Barbie doll clothes left lying around the shag.

Brenda pokes her head through the kitchen doorway.

"Do you know what they have in the basement?" she asks mischievously, then disappears back into the kitchen.

Intrigued, the twins follow Brenda down the basement steps, Hope nearly tripping over Gladys, who dashes down into the darkness.

The Gehrigs' is a large old cellar of painted but uneven cement walls and floor, used mainly for storage. Brenda stands by a washer/dryer set, scooping handfuls of coins out of a jug.

Hope and Joy look at each other.

"We'll go to Cook's after and buy candy," she says.

"It'll be closed today," Joy says.

"So, we'll keep the money until we can go," Brenda counters, annoyed.

Joy wanders toward the darker recesses of the basement. She fingers the dust on a large trunk freezer, unplugged and hiding in a corner.

"What is this?" Hope asks.

Not far from the washer/dryer sits a disused piece of exercise equipment. It's the kind of thing you'd see in an old sitcom. It looks like a doctor's office scale, but one with a belt meant to vibrate fat away.

"Cool…" Brenda notes.

"How does it work?" Joy wonders, examining it.

Hope stands on it.

"Me first," Brenda demands.

Hope steps off. Brenda stands on the platform, ducks inside the belt, and looks for an 'on' button. The machine fires up, the belt vibrating little Brenda Cassidy, who talks and laughs. Her voice sounds like voices do when you speak into the blades of a fan.

Hope bends her head over the knobs that keep the belt vibrating, back and forth and back and forth almost too rapidly to see the motion. As she leans in, one knob grabs her hair, and she is immediately pinned to the machine, her hair wound around the still working knob.

"Turn it off! Turn it off! TURN IT OFF!"

Joy pushes the button, and the roaring monster quiets.

Hope can feel the cold metal of the machine against her scalp. She twists helplessly at the knob and panics.

Joy and Brenda look on, shaken. They circle the machine, staring silently. Brenda inches backward.

Joy reaches in, tries to unwind Hope's hair from the machine.

"Ow!"

She tries to unscrew the knob, but her small hands slip.

There's a long silence, and then Brenda, backing up the basement steps, whispers, "Let's go. Come on. Let's just go."

Attached by the head to a machine at least twice her weight, stooped to one side and crying, Hope stares, too bewildered to even beg them not to go. She watches, sobbing, as Joy joins Brenda on the steps.

The bare bulb over the washer/dryer casts wobbly shadows as the little girls run up the wooden stairs. A third shadow, though, does not ascend the steps.

Hope's head swims. She tries to look around the basement, but her head is so tightly fixed to the machine that she can look only in one direction: toward the shadow in the corner.

It grows, begins to take shape.

Hope tugs desperately at the caught hair, wriggling sideways to see what might be approaching from behind her.

She gives up, looks back into the corner at a shape now looming up the entire wall.

Are those wings?

Hope covers her eyes and wails. The sound spooks Gladys, who darts in front of the shadow and up the stairs.

The sun seems very bright as the two girls burst out the Gehrigs' kitchen door. Brenda takes off toward home, and Gladys jets to freedom. Joy walks deliberately next door.

Her parents are both on the phone. Her mom sits on a battered yellow kitchen chair, absently fingering the violets her husband picked for her this morning and talking to Aunt Helen from back home.

Maureen Murphy is respectable in that tight-lipped, elbow grease kind of way. Humble but formidable and deeply decent, she is a lovely woman, but world-wearied and skinny—bony, really—with snow-white hair turned much too young. She is quick with a stern glance or word, slow with a compliment, but loving. For the Murphys, she is security, not the smell of baking bread. She is sheer will, savvy, and Formula 409.

Mr. Murphy is in the next room, sitting on a rolling office chair near his desk, strewn with speakers, wires, and trophy parts, including several victory angels lying prone on stacks of papers. He has the second phone up to his ear, but he's not talking.

Joy walks quietly up to her father.

"Come with me," she says soberly. "Bring your tools."

Mr. Murphy quietly sets the receiver on his desk, pulls out a large, wide drawer, grabs his tool belt, and walks out the front door to avoid drawing the attention of his wife in the kitchen. Joy leads him silently to the Gehrigs' unlocked back door, then down the basement steps.

Hope sobs violently, shielding her face and repeating, "I don't want to...I don't want to..."

"Calm down," her dad tells her with a lilt of compassion.

She sees him and sobs more violently, out of relief as much as anything.

Joy stands quietly behind him.

"Quiet, quiet," he part lulls, part reprimands.

James Murphy tilts Hope's head, though there is precious little give. He eyes the rotators, pulls a screwdriver from his belt, and dismantles the machine.

A pitiable creature, her hair tangled to about 1/3 its natural length on the right side of her head, Hope stands red-faced and out of breath. Her dad pats her hair, kisses her forehead, and leaving the broken piece of work-out equipment behind him, leads both girls up the basement stairs.

"Let's go, chickadees."

Hope buries her face in her dad's side.

Joy trails one stair step behind. She stands, staring, as her dad and her twin sister reach the kitchen. Looking into the darkness, Joy smiles, then waves.

Monday, the Day After Easter

"OK, but let's not go see Brenda," Hope says, still a little stung from yesterday. "Let's see if Kelly Parkins can play."

The girls would rather stay inside and watch TV, but Mrs. Murphy is cleaning, and Hope and Joy are not to get underfoot.

Our Lady of Perpetual Help Elementary School is closed today, the last day of Easter break. Hope and Joy sit twisting on backyard swings in light sweaters, Hope eyeballing a large, squawky group of blackbirds harassing the unkempt lilac bush.

The girls' older sister Hannah, a high school sophomore, passes them on her way to her job at Coney Castle, a soft-serve ice cream stand a few blocks away.

"Will you bring home chip wheelies?" Hope calls after her.

Hannah doesn't answer.

Bored, the girls cross the back road and walk up the "grass alley," the meeting of unfenced backyards behind a string of neighborhood houses. They head toward the willow tree that hangs over the Parkins yard.

The Parkinses have an A-frame clubhouse in their backyard that Mr. Parkins built. Hope and Joy check inside the empty clubhouse for their friend before trying the house. Hope sees Brenda Cassidy's red kickball and worries she may already be here.

Approaching the open back door, the girls see Mrs. Parkins in the kitchen mopping the floor.

"Hi, twinset," she says through the screen. "Go around front. Kelly's on the porch."

As they often do, Joy and Hope cut through the garage. Mr. Parkins, a small man with a high-pitched voice and severely combed hair, stands off to one side with his tackle box and a dirty Styrofoam cooler.

"Hiya, girls," he chirps.

The girls nod and fight the urge to run.

"Hey, Kelly!" he shouts to his daughter out front. "Come on back. I have a surprise for everyone."

Mr. Parkins stands beaming in his pressed white undershirt and white pants. He smiles and nods at the Murphy girls, then claps his hands.

"Get a move on, Kelly," he trills. And then, conspiratorially to the twins, he says, "If she's not back here lickity-split, guess I'll just have to share my surprise with you two, and she'll be left out."

Kelly Parkins lopes into the garage.

"Looky here," Mr. Parkins says. "The Murphy girls are visiting. Just in time, too."

He smiles and opens his cooler. All three girls peek inside at four twitching fish piled on dirty ice chips.

"I caught them this morning," Mr. Parkins tells the girls with a teacherly tone. "Now, do you girls know how to clean a fish?"

Kelly Parkins shrugs. Hope and Joy stand silent.

"Well, you're going to learn today."

Mr. Parkins pulls a silver fish about twice as long as his hand from the brown-speckled ice and slaps it on a cutting board on the worktable in front of him.

"You put a little cut right under his head," Mr. Parkins explains, picking up a short knife from the table next to his cutting board. He slices a notch into the fish beneath its head. The fish flaps on the cutting board.

Hope shudders. Mr. Parkins smiles.

"He's still alive," Hope says.

"Now you gut him," Mr. Parkins continues, "by slicing down his belly."

He slits the fish from notch to tip.

"He's still alive," Hope whispers again, taking a step back.

"Then cut the head through the other side—"

He gouges another notch beneath the top of the fish's head.

"And when you rip, the guts come out with the head."

Mr. Parkins demonstrates, pulling the fish's head loose from the body, its spine and set of organs intact.

"He's alive," Hope whispers.

Kelly and Joy stare blankly at Mr. Parkins. He giggles.

"And that's how it's done," Mr. Parkins says with satisfaction. He pulls a second fish from the cooler. "Who wants to try this guy?"

"Can I get a drink of water?" Hope asks.

"Sure can, no prob," Mr. Parkins tells her as Joy steps toward the table, and Kelly takes the knife from her dad.

Hope runs for the kitchen door. Her feet slide a bit on the wet linoleum as she makes her way to the refrigerator. She spies a fresh pitcher of red Kool-Aid. The Murphys never make Kool-Aid.

She looks around. There's no one to ask. She decides to have a drink and pulls the full pitcher from the shelf. It's heavy and wet, and she loses her grip.

Hope drops the pitcher, spilling the entire contents of red on the freshly cleaned floor.

She stands, staring.

Mrs. Parkins appears and shakes her head.

"Oh, Hope," she frowns, tossing dish towels down to sop up the mess and mutters, "and I just washed it…"

Hope backs out the door and into the garage. Mr. Parkins passes her in the doorway.

Hope stands, half in and half out of the garage. She stares red-faced and worried toward her sister.

"What did you do?" Joy asks. She looks so tiny and unhappy. She balls her fists and asks Hope again, "What did you do?"

Mr. Parkins yells from the house.

"Well, my word!"

"You're in trouble," Kelly Parkins says with some sympathy.

Hope walks into the cool dark of the garage and moves slowly toward her sister, but the closer she gets, the stronger the fish odor. She sees the table and the spotted Styrofoam and feels she may retch.

Mr. Parkins returns.

"That's it, Murphy girls," he announces. "You're grounded."

Hope and Joy stare silently. Kelly slinks out of the garage.

"You heard me," he says. "Now go."

Hope and Joy walk glumly through the garage and the backyard, heading toward the grass alley. Instead of taking it straight toward home, they turn right and move toward the Cassidys' place, but Mr. Parkins yells behind them.

"Oh no, you don't! I said grounded, and that means home."

Joy and Hope turn and look at him, baffled.

"Don't go see Brenda," Mr. Parkins demands. "That's where we're going."

He turns to his daughter.

"Come on, Kel-Kel. Let's go visit Brenda."

Joy looks at Hope, who's staring at the ground.

"You're not listening," he snaps. "I said home."

They stand and stare.

"Go home," he says again.

They turn toward home.

"I don't think he can do that," Joy says quietly.

The two trudge back up the grass alley toward 93 Second Ave.

"We won't be allowed inside," Hope complains.

"We don't want to tell Mom, anyway."

Back in their own yard, each sister takes a perch on a backyard swing, twisting the chains unhappily. They sing:

Little bird, little bird

Little beak, little squeak

Fuzzy throat, little peep

Chick, chick, chick, chick, chickadee

Birds lift from the willow down the grass alley, and the girls watch as Kelly and her dad walk up the way toward them, then turn toward the Cassidys'. Shortly,

Brenda, Kelly, and Mr. Parkins—striding triumphantly—pass the unmerry Murphy backyard.

"Look there, girls," he says to Brenda and Kelly. "The Murphy girls think being grounded means playing in your backyard. I don't think it does. Do you?"

Kelly Parkins shakes her head.

"No. It means sitting in your room and thinking about what you've done," Brenda says.

"That's right, Brendie," Mr. Parkins agrees, stroking the girl's head proudly.

The three come to a dramatic halt at the edge of the Murphy property and wait for Hope and Joy to comply.

The Murphy girls stare back without moving.

"Well…" Mr. Parkins says.

Nothing.

Mr. Parkins stomps a foot.

Wings rustle in the lilac bush. Joy pushes her swing back and picks up her feet. Hope stares motionless at Mr. Parkins.

Eventually, Mr. Parkins sighs irritably and ushers his charges down the grass alley toward the willow and A-frame clubhouse.

Gladys rubs against Hope's foot. She squats down to rub her head, and Joy joins her.

"She's probably hungry," Joy says. "We should feed her."

Hope eyes the Gehrig's house and shudders.

Joy scoops up the cat and marches right in the back door they never bothered locking. Hope takes a few steps after her sister, thinks better of it, and takes her chances inside 93 Second.

Hours later, Little House on the Prairie is on TV, which means Hope and Joy should already be in bed. Spring break is officially over. It ended with a dull thud for the Murphy twins. Tomorrow is another school day. It's one Hope, in particular, isn't looking forward to. She brushes her teeth slowly and hopes to psychically convince her parents to keep her home in the morning.

She groans quietly, looks toward her parents and handsome Michael Landon, then tries again a little louder. No one notices. She sighs, then she clutches at her stomach, walking slowly toward the living room when the phone rings.

Mrs. Murphy walks past Hope to pick up the kitchen phone.

Hope lets go of her stomach and drops her head, defeated. She'll have to be more convincing in the morning.

"Hello?"

Mrs. Murphy looks toward Hope.

"We haven't seen her, Carol," Mrs. Murphy replies. "Hang on one second."

Mrs. Murphy motions to Hope.

"Hope, did you two play with Brenda Cassidy today?"

Embarrassed, Hope shakes her head no.

"Sorry, Carol," Mrs. Murphy says. "She hasn't been here. Did you try the Parkinses?"

Pause. Mrs. Murphy shakes her head.

"Good luck. Call and let us know if you need help looking."

Mrs. Murphy hangs up the phone and gives her daughter an unexpected hug.

"Up to bed now, chickadee," Mrs. Murphy says. "We have to get to school early tomorrow."

Tuesday After Easter Break

The twins sit in a shiny, well-lit hallway outside the Our Lady of Perpetual Help Elementary School administrative office. Joy's thick waves hold tight in a long braid, where Hope's thinner, straighter locks are already sliding free. Inside, their mother talks with Mrs. Marinis, the school's kind, but firm, principal.

Hope squirms in her chair, ducking as a bee bobs her way and then into the office across the hall.

"It's actually common practice with twins, Mrs. Murphy."

"Is it?" Mrs. Murphy is skeptical.

"Sr. Cleofa thinks it's time," Mrs. Marinis continues. "Research says it's better for both siblings. By separating your girls into different classrooms, each will have her own opportunity to develop and learn."

"They'd rather be together. It helps them feel safe."

Mrs. Marinis pauses.

"Oh, poor little Brenda is your neighbor, isn't she?" Mrs. Marinis squeezes Mrs. Murphy's hand and shakes her head. "The new sheriff is actually due here this morning to look around."

"The new sheriff is a jackass."

"We're all shaken by the little Cassidy girl's disappearance. Your twins, well, they're probably frightened and worried. Still, first grade is the time to help them develop independent personalities. Let's not put this off."

She pauses. Mrs. Murphy's face is stony.

"It will do them both good—especially Joy. She's so quiet, Mrs. Murphy. This will give her the chance to blossom without Hope interfering."

"Can't it wait until the beginning of the next school year?" Mrs. Murphy asks. "Why move Joy now?"

"Sr. Cleofa is adamant that she have Hope alone."

Mrs. Murphy grimaces.

"Joy leans on Hope quite a bit," Mrs. Marinis presses. "This will give Joy the chance to take care of herself, instead of letting Hope do all the work."

"I think you may have that backward."

"It will do wonders to bring her out of her shell," Mrs. Marinis says. "Sr. Angela's very nurturing and kind."

"And Hope?"

Slight pause.

"I know Sr. Cleofa is a little more old-fashioned, but I think Hope will benefit from the discipline."

The pink-cheeked school secretary enters.

"So sorry to interrupt," she says. "The police are here."

"Thank you, Mrs. Brickner." Marinis braces herself, glancing into the outer office at the new sheriff. "Please tell him I will be with him in just a minute."

She looks grimly toward Mrs. Murphy.

"It is awful."

Maureen Murphy nods. Marinis shakes her head.

"I just can't believe something like this could happen in Odenton."

Mrs. Murphy isn't sure why Odenton should be so unusual. There are people in every neighborhood on earth who weaken and thrill at the idea of ruining something innocent. She doesn't have all the details, though. She doesn't know that, as she and Mrs. Marinis speak, Mrs. Parkins is discovering the little neighbor girl, her small, green sneaker poking out at a very wrong angle from the playhouse doorway. The girl is ripped right up the center, her face slack and grey like something made of putty.

"It's usually someone the children know, isn't that right?" Mrs. Murphy supposes.

"But cults and covens…"

"That's nonsense. When something is too ugly for people to understand, they look for answers that make them feel safe when they should be looking for the truth."

The women exit the office. Gaietto has moved from the outer office to the sun-streaked hallway, nodding at the Murphy twins. He pats Joy on the head.

"Keep an extra eye on these two," he says, winking at Mrs. Murphy, then leans in close to the little girls. "And be aware of Satan's schemes, that he may not outwit us."

Mrs. Murphy pushes past the sheriff and takes each girl by the hand. As they walk the shining halls of OLPH, the click of Maureen Murphy's conservative pumps echo through the corridors. No child art adorns these walls, but a large crucifix faces every stairway. Mrs. Murphy bends, kisses Joy on the head, and points to a classroom door. A cardboard sign decorates its window, painted with holy doves and streaming light, reading, "Sr. Angela's Classroom."

Joy looks at her sister. She drops her head and tugs the door open. A lithe nun in light blue approaches, puts her hand on Joy's shoulder, waves to Mrs. Murphy, and guides Joy into the classroom.

A stout, short, older nun in full black regalia enters the hall from the room opposite Sr. Angela's.

"We can't be tardy, regardless of the situation," Sr. Cleofa states.

Mrs. Murphy sighs.

"Have a good day, chickadee," she says to Hope.

Hope hesitates. Sr. Cleofa taps a yardstick on the smooth floor. The cracking noise makes Hope jump. She reluctantly follows the old nun into her classroom.

The room is tidy. No children's art is displayed here, either. Hope takes her seat about halfway back, in the center of the room. Brenda Cassidy's seat sits vacant near the window, but Hope's gaze is fixed on the empty desk next to her own.

The nun pads quietly to face her students.

"Did the Easter bunny pay everyone a visit?" Cleofa asks a silent classroom.

No response.

"Hmm?" she asks again, pacing between rows. She stops next to Hope's desk.

"Did the Easter bunny visit the Murphy house?" she asks.

Hope recognizes this as a trick question but does not know the correct answer, so she says nothing.

"Answer me."

Hope stares past the nun toward the window, watches the shadows of birds dancing in the spring sun.

"I see," Cleofa grumbles. "Not so talkative without your twin around."

She spins to address all twenty-seven six-and seven-year-olds.

"There is no Easter bunny," she announces. "He is a figure created, based on pagan ritual, to allow non-Christians to steal our holiest of days."

Silence.

She stalks to the front of the classroom and soaks in the wide-eyed shock in her pupils' faces.

"Why is Easter our holiest of days? Why not Christmas?" she asks twenty-seven terrified children.

No one answers, and Cleofa sighs disgustedly.

"Dennis, what does Christmas signify?"

The blond with the crooked mouth blinks back tears.

"Come, come," she reprimands him. "Why do we celebrate Christmas?"

"It's Jesus's birthday," he offers meekly.

"Correct," she tells the relieved boy. "And why is that less important than Easter—Molly?"

A curly-haired brunette sitting not far from Hope stammers.

"Because…" Cleofa ambles toward Molly, who sputters, "I…I…um..."

"I…I…I," Cleofa mocks her. "Because everyone is born, Molly Gross. Only our Lord was resurrected."

Cleofa walks toward a small boy a few desks away.

"Do you know what that means, Robbie Scherger?"

"No," the boy says plainly.

"It means He came back to life from the dead."

"Like a zombie?" Robbie asks.

Several children laugh, but it's clear to Hope that Robbie is not making a joke. Hope has never thought of Jesus as a zombie before, but Sr. Cleofa's story makes it sound right. However, it doesn't seem to be a question Cleofa wants to hear. After a brief, red-faced pause, Cleofa points dramatically toward the classroom door and yells.

"Robbie Scherger, you go tell Mrs. Marinis that you took the Lord's name in vain, and you disrespected our Savior!"

There's a great squawking, like laughter, from the birds outside the window. Hope wants badly to lay her head on her wobbly desk pad.

After school, Hope and Joy meet in the hallway between their classrooms. They wait quietly for Joannie Fabrizio, the eighth grader and neighbor who walks them home every day.

Sister Angela closes her classroom door behind her, turns to the girls, and says, "Have a blessed afternoon, Murphy twins."

She looks up and smiles at a figure behind Joy and Hope.

"Sister Angela," Sr. Cleofa frowns as she says it.

"I'll see you all tomorrow," Sr. Angela says as she glides down the stairs.

Beyond them, the elevator door opens.

Again, Sister Cleofa frowns.

"Did you two do that?" she asks.

Joy and Hope stare bewildered at each other.

"You're not to touch the button," she scolds. "It's broken."

Sister Cleofa parts the sisters to walk toward the gaping elevator shaft.

"Hmm," she wonders with irritation.

A dark shadow falls across the hallway as birds begin flapping wildly outside the nearby window.

Sr. Cleofa holds the wall with one hand and unsteadily peers into the abyss.

Birds caw and cackle, their action making a massive, writhing shadow that jumps and leaps.

Sr. Cleofa lingers for what seems a long time.

Hope stares.

Cleofa leans. Hope sees the old woman's little hands gripping the wall, her small shoes peeking out from under the black skirt.

Suddenly the nun pulls herself backward.

"Can't imagine what's gotten into those birds."

She turns to the girls.

"Are you planning to loiter in my hallway all afternoon?"

Joy points. She can see Joannie walking toward them from the eighth-grade wing, her hair a tight set of curls, the OLPH on her cheerleading uniform spattered with chocolate milk.

Sr. Cleofa grumbles and lumbers back into her classroom.

"Hey, losers," Joannie smiles. "You ready?"

They grab their matching Scooby-Doo book bags from the floor and follow Joannie toward Sandusky Street and home.

"Do you know what happened to Brenda Cassidy?" Joannie asks them.

"She's gone," Joy says.

"Yeah, but do you know what happened to her?" Joannie asks mischievously.

"What?" Hope wants to know.

"Wouldn't you like to know?" Joannie teases.

Two other eighth graders coast past Joy and Hope on bikes, rolling to a stop near Joannie.

"Hey!" Joannie cheers. She trots ahead to join her friends. They walk their bikes and talk to Joannie, who, in turn, ignores the Murphy girls all the way home, except to say, loudly enough to draw their attention, "They're probably scared they'll be next!"

She laughs and turns, walking backward and smiling at Joy and Hope.

"Who'd bother with turds like them, though? They are totally safe!"

Joannie and her friends laugh.

Joy and Hope walk behind, mindlessly singing:

Come be with me

Come play with me

We'll go, you'll see

Secret place, you and me

Chickadee

The three older kids look at each other and then back at the twins.

"God, they are creepy," Joanie whispers.

The three laugh nervously. The two on bikes peel off halfway up Short Street, an eyeshot from the Cassidys' backyard. Those remaining walk silently past, eyes downcast, then bolt up the back road to the Fabrizios'.

All three drop their bags inside the kitchen door.

"Let's sit on the porch," Joannie says, grabbing a bag of Tootsie Rolls from the kitchen counter. "We can have a snack."

They walk through the Fabrizios' immaculate living room onto a screened-in front porch with newish furniture.

"You guys should bring Hannah's Cars album over so I can borrow it," Joanie tells the girls.

"We're not allowed to touch Hannah's records," Hope reports.

"Honey Gehrig has it, too," Joy tells her.

"So? She's not going to lend it to me. And how would you know?"

"We fed the cat yesterday," Hope says quietly.

"Besides, they're still gone," Joanie remembers.

"Til tomorrow," Joy says. "But the door's unlocked still."

"What?"

"We forgot to lock it," Hope admits. "They have lots of records, plus they have a big bucket of change on the washer."

"Did you steal?!" Joanie accuses, smiling.

"No!" Hope denies it.

"I bet you did, Hope," Joanie says, leaning toward her.

"I didn't."

"Not Joy, though," Joanie says, stroking Joy's head. "Joy's a good girl."

Joannie hands Joy a tootsie roll. Hope looks on, envious.

"I know what happened to Brenda Cassidy," Joannie says, popping a Tootsie Roll into her mouth.

Joannie pulls little Joy onto a cushioned porch swing, and they sit together, rummaging through the brown and orange plastic bag of Tootsie Rolls. Long, gangly Hope sits on the porch floor, facing them and looking unhappy.

"Can I have a Tootsie Roll?"

Joannie ignores her.

"Everybody knows what really happened to Brenda," Joannie says. "It was Bloody Fingers."

Bloody Fingers is a boogeyman story Hope and Joy's older sister Hannah sometimes told Joannie to scare her when she was a kid. Now, Joannie—too young to be Hannah's friend, too old to be Hope and Joy's friend—uses it to scare the girls.

"You know what that means," Joannie whispers. "Brenda probably heard him coming."

Joannie smiles.

Hope holds her breath.

"Thump.....thump.....draaaaagggg...Bloody Fingers on the first step."

"Stop it," Hope says.

"Thump....thump....draaaaggggg...."

"Stop..." Hope says more urgently.

Joy isn't afraid. She digs quietly into the bag of snacks on Joannie's lap. Meanwhile, Joannie watches Hope's increasing terror with glee.

"Bloody Fingers on the second step..."

Hope hides her face with her hands. Joannie silently sides off the swing, opens the front porch door, pulls

Hope up from the floor, and pushes her off the porch. Joannie closes and locks the screen door.

She returns to the swing and Joy, who diverts her eyes from Hope's silent pleas.

"Go home," Joannie says.

Hope says nothing. She doesn't yell or cry or breathe.

"Isn't this candy delicious?" Joannie asks Joy.

Joy looks sadly at her sister but doesn't say anything. Hope, meanwhile, pulls desperately at the door.

"Go home, Hope," Joannie says. Then, "Oh, no, Joy—do you see it? Can you hear it?"

And it begins.

"Thump...." Joannie slides off the swing, crouches low, and begins moving toward the screen door and Hope.

"No! No, no, no, no, no, no..." Hope pleads.

"Thump..."

"Stop it! Stop it! Let me in!!"

"Draaaaag"

"Waaaahhhhhh!!"

Pound, pound, pound. Sob, sob, sob.

Hope puts her hands over her eyes doing her best to avoid visual knowledge of the maniacal Bloody Fingers, who could at this very second be on the bottom of the three steps on which she is standing.

Joannie waits a few minutes, then unlatches the door.

"Oh, come in, you big baby."

She tosses some Tootsie Rolls to Hope, who does not manage to catch them. The red-faced, snotty, tear-streaked mess gathers the candy from the porch floor and joins her sister on the bench swing.

Less than an hour passes before Mr. Murphy knocks on the screen door.

"Hello, Mr. Murphy," Joannie smiles.

"You two ready?"

He gives both girls a squeeze. Joannie fetches their bags, and the three Murphys cut across the Gehrigs' yard toward their own back door. Their kitchen rings with happy voices. Bridget, the girls' oldest sister, is home.

Bridget is larger-than-life. Tall and statuesque with an over-eager smile, she commands attention. She talks and laughs loudly and easily. She's beautiful, with thick, dark waves and a strong, curvy build that makes you think of Wonder Woman.

Bridget lives on the other side of town in an apartment—really the ground floor of an old, large home that's been remodeled to accommodate Odenton's modest post-college population. Her shiny new degree is in communication, and the sheriff has tapped her to help him document his ongoing investigation into Odenton's occult activity.

"The sheriff asked me to work with him on it," she's saying to her mother in the kitchen.

"The sheriff is a jackass," Mrs. Murphy says for the second time today.

"Mom!" Bridget is equally impressed and offended.

"What he's saying is horseshit," Mr. Murphy agrees. He sets the twins' book bags under the kitchen table and kisses his eldest daughter on the head. "Ignore him, Bridget. Everyone should just ignore him."

Hannah comes up the basement steps, laundry basket in hand.

Hannah is the hard candy shell to Bridget's sweet, chewy insides. She determines the girls' chores, chides them into brushing their teeth, and trains them to hurl insults and scrub bathtub scum.

"Gaietto is a joke," Hannah confirms. "Did you see the objectionable album burning in the Gazette?"

Hannah pantomimes air quotes for emphasis.

"Big picture of the bonfire. A Jim Croce album is the one you can see burning. Jim's big face about to go up," she laughs. "Because Jim Croce is so objectionable!"

"A little girl is missing, and what is our sheriff doing? He's looking for witches!" Mrs. Murphy says. "It just means he isn't looking for the real problem. If I were Carol Cassidy, I'd be fit to be tied! It's probably someone they know, probably that uncle."

"Now, hon," Mr. Murphy looks at his wife disapprovingly.

"I don't know," Bridget says. "People really seem to think he knows what he's talking about. He's going to be on Geraldo!"

"Good grief!" Hannah echoes her parents' thoughts.

"The devil made me do it just gives everyone in town the chance to absolve themselves of responsibility," Mrs. Murphy grumbles.

"Or target whoever they don't like," Hannah offers bitterly.

"Can we play outside until supper?" Joy asks.

"No!" Bridget says. "It's not safe."

"Yes," Mrs. Murphy corrects. "Don't leave the yard."

Joy and Hope sit on the front porch.

"I wish Bridget came to take us to a movie or the park or something," Hope laments.

"Maybe we can go to Coney Castle after supper," Joy hopes.

"I wish she was talking about anything else," Hope says.

"Don't be a baby. What should we do?"

"Play hide and seek?"

It's Hope's idea, so Joy is the first to count. Joy hides her face in her hands and singsongs, "Five, ten, fifteen, twenty…"

Hope slips off the porch and rounds the house. She hears flapping around back, sees a shadow. Spooked, she sneaks up to the covered stairway alongside the Gehrigs' house, the one that leads to the apartment upstairs, and hides.

But it's dark. And it feels like it's taking so long—hours. And it really is dark – dark like the Gehrig basement. Hope abandons her spot and runs back to the front porch.

No Joy.

Hope yells.

"Joy! Joy! Come out!"

She can't find her sister, who's not even the one who's supposed to be hiding. Hope looks inside the lilac bush. She rounds the house and looks out back. She circles around again and sits, dejected, on the front porch steps.

"Joy!" she yells. "I said come out!"

Joy rounds the side of the house.

"You don't tell me to come out. You're hiding. Knucklehead."

"I quit."

"Fine," Joy drones. "What now, then?"

"Do you think you can walk around under Gehrigs' porch?" Hope wonders aloud. "Like the porch floor is a ceiling if you're underneath it, with dirt for a floor?"

"I don't know," Joy says.

"We should find out."

The two walk toward their next-door neighbors' large front porch, flanked on both sides by tall, unkempt bushes. The two kids push through the branches on the Murphy side of the porch, hear peeping from a nest high above them, discover that the lattice that covers the space from the porch floor to the ground is easily wrenched far enough to allow two skinny girls to wiggle through. They find themselves exploring the dirt below the Gehrigs' front porch.

They play for a while, but Hope's too tall to stand and has to crawl on her knees. Joy can stand if she bends her head far to one side. Eventually, they decide they're uncomfortable and want to go back home.

But the blue jay has returned to the nest in the unruly bush.

Hope crawls from the dirt, squeezing past the lattice only to have a very angry bird dive at her, cawing. She screams, pushes Joy back under the porch, and squeezes back under herself.

"There's a mean bird," she tells her sister. "He won't let me out."

Joy peeks through the lattice. She sees only twigs, branches, and dirt, but she hears the bird.

"It's just a bird.".

She pushes the lattice and pokes her head out, but the bird dives toward her, and she jumps back under the porch.

They hear their mom calling them for dinner.

"Mom!" Hope hollers.

"Ssshhh!" Joy says. "We'll get in trouble. We should try again. We'll just run as fast as we can right to our porch."

Joy pushes all the way out but running is tough because she has to maneuver her way through the bush, and the bird won't let her. It caws and dives, and quickly Joy is back under the porch.

Mom is calling. Hope is crying.

"Over here, girls."

They hear a man's voice from the far end of the porch. He doesn't sound like anyone they know, but he does sound familiar. They can't see him, but there's a light where he's removed part of the lattice.

Hope hesitates.

"No…"

Joy marches across the dirt, stooped but determined, and Hope crawls behind her.

They get close.

Hope won't look. She grabs the back of Joy's shirt, squeezes her eyes shut, and follows Joy out the opening left by strange hands.

Bridget is calling.

"Hope and Joy!"

She drags out the second name like it's longer than it is: Joe-why.

Hope looks only at her feet, and the girls dash around Gehrigs' front yard to their own.

"Mom said not to leave the yard, you two!" Bridget reprimands. "I won't tell, but this is serious. Right now, you have to be extra careful. Don't talk to anybody you don't know. Make sure someone knows where you are at all times."

She notices tear marks smeared through the dirt on Hope's face.

"Are you all right?"

"We got trapped under their porch," Joy explains, pointing.

"What?!"

"There's a mean bird. He wouldn't let us out," Joy continues.

"Oh, sweetie pies!" Bridget scoops them into an embrace. "There's probably a mama bird protecting a nest. Were you so scared?"

They were.

She hugs them closer, then leads them around the side of the house toward the lilac bush and the kitchen door beyond it. As they open the back door, they hear a knock around front. Mrs. Murphy pushes back the well-worn yellow kitchen chair and passes through the living room to answer.

"Jo, how are you?" Mrs. Murphy asks, opening the door to Mrs. Fabrizio. Mr. Fabrizio stands behind her, scratching his arms on the shadowy porch.

"Oh, Maureen, did you hear?" Jo Fabrizio asks, leaning through the door and taking Mrs. Murphy's hands.

"Shame," Mr. Fabrizio says behind his wife. "Real shame."

Mrs. Murphy steps through the doorway onto the porch without closing the front door.

Hope walks through the living room.

"Hon!" Mrs. Murphy yells into the house.

James Murphy passes Hope and joins his wife in the doorway.

"In that clubhouse he built," Mrs. Fabrizio repeats.

"Cut her to pieces," Mr. Fabrizio says.

Hope walks closer.

"Heya, kiddo," Mr. Fabrizio says through the door. "You haven't seen Joannie, have you?"

Hope shakes her head.

"She's–" Maureen Murphy starts nervously.

"Oh, it's fine," Mr. Fabrizio says. "Out with her pals, probably."

"Just makes you jumpy," his wife finishes.

She gives Mrs. Murphy's hand a squeeze, and she and her husband descend the porch steps.

"Go wash your hands for supper," Mr. Murphy tells Hope. "Where's your sister?"

All four Murphy girls are standing in the living room.

"Um…right here," Hannah says, pointing around her.

"Go wash up," he says again.

Hope turns toward the bathroom. Joy joins her.

"Since when do we wash up before supper?"

"They got it from Little House," Joy decides.

"What are we eating?"

"Something gross."

They lather up with Coast deodorant soap and follow an unappealing smell into the kitchen.

"Chipped beef," Joy predicts.

"Gaietto's getting bolder. This is—well, this is insane," Mrs. Murphy is saying, loading chipped beef in creamy sauce onto dry toast. Hope and Joy groan and take their seats.

"People believe what they want to believe," Mr. Murphy responds. "It makes them feel safe."

"It makes them feel superior," Mrs. Murphy corrects him.

"What if it really is something to do with Satanic worship?" Bridget is saying to her parents.

"A squirrely neighborhood dad did something unspeakable," Mrs. Murphy whispers. "And the devil was there, that's for sure, but not with robes and goat heads and whatever nonsense."

"What did Mrs. Fabrizio say the sheriff told her?" Bridget reminds her mother. "Gaietto says he had the horns of Baphomet hanging as a symbol in his workroom."

"The horns of—good lord, Bridget. The man was a hunter. Those horns could have been from anything."

Mrs. Murphy is quickly tiring of this conversation.

"And now Joannie's gone missing?" Bridget says, eyebrow raised.

"She's not at home. That doesn't mean she's missing," her father corrects her.

"What happened?" Hope asks.

"Nothing, sweetheart," Dad says.

Mrs. Murphy looks at her girls for a minute.

"Hope and Joy, did Mr. Parkins ever seem weird to you?" Bridget asks.

"All the time," Hope says.

"He grounded us yesterday," Joy says.

Hope looks at her, stricken.

"He what?!" Bridget yelps.

"Hope accidentally spilled juice on their kitchen floor, and he grounded us," Joy responds.

"He can't do that!" Bridget says with shock.

"He did," Hope says, now courageous. "And we came home, and we were going to go to the Cassidys', but he told us not to because we were grounded and weren't allowed to leave our backyard, and then they went and got Brenda and said they were going to get ice cream."

The kitchen goes silent.

"It's a good thing he sent you home," Mr. Murphy says, reaching for Joy and pulling her close to him.

"Mr. Parkins killed Brenda," Mrs. Murphy says plainly to her children. "It probably happened that same day."

Bridget hugs Hope, the closest twin.

The kitchen is tiny, tight, and quiet.

No one has much appetite for chipped beef.

The next morning, Mrs. Murphy hangs up the phone. She whispers to her husband, who gets up off the couch and pulls on a jacket.

"You're taking us to school today?" Hope asks. She looks at Joy, relieved they won't walk to school with Joannie today. She's still mad and embarrassed.

"Yeah," Mr. Murphy says quietly. "You're coming with me today, chickadees."

As the Murphys walk out the back door and toward their green station wagon sitting on the edge of their little yard, Paulette Stimmell and Honey Gehrig are standing next door watching police lights bounce around the Fabrizios' backyard.

"You haven't lived here long enough to know, so I am telling you," Paulette stage whispers. "When their birthday falls on Easter, terrible things happen in this town.

Book 3: Chicks
1982

Sunday before Easter

Joy and Hope will turn twelve in one week on Easter Sunday. During this holy week leading up to the girls' birthday and their Lord's resurrection, they will make the next in a line of Roman Catholic sacraments.

They've been through several of the Church's Big Seven already: baptism, holy Eucharist, and that oh-so Catholic ritual of confessing your sins and seeking forgiveness, reconciliation.

Now confirmation is coming, the day the girls will personally claim their places as Catholics.

They've been studying. They've learned the difference between menial and mortal sin. They had to align someone they knew with each of the twelve fruits of the Holy Spirit: charity, joy, peace, patience, benignity, goodness, longsuffering, mildness, faith, modesty, continence, and chastity.

No hope.

They chose confirmation names.

Now, as they get ready for Mass, their family pools around the living room at 93 Second.

James Murphy tosses the wilting wild violets from his wife's plump little vase, changes the water, and squeezes in a new handful. The knees of his pants are still damp from picking.

Aunt Helen is in from Philadelphia for Easter. She's like a sweeter, more delicate version of the girls' mom. Her adult daughter Debbie, toting 6-year-old Shaun, is with her. Debbie and Shaun will head back to Philly tomorrow, but Helen's staying through Easter.

Of course, Hannah is on hand. She's home from college for Easter break, working at the Coney Castle, and complaining that the girls aren't keeping the house clean.

Bridget will meet everyone at the church.

"This is way better than First Communion," Hope notes to her twin as they pull their new peasant skirts from the hangars in their bedroom closet. "I hated those veils. That was so weird."

"Like we were marrying Jesus," Joy points out.

"Why would Jesus want to marry a bunch of second graders?" Hope wonders.

"This is better than first confession, too."

"I hated that so much," Hope winces. "I just made stuff up. I was afraid I would bore Fr. Bowersox."

"He's a sinner, too."

Joy points toward Hope's bed to a copy of A Lector Prepares, a workbook full of mass readings and hints on the proper way to deliver The Word.

"You going to look that over?"

Hope shrugs.

"I shouldn't have to be a reader the same day I make my confirmation," she complains. "One or the other."

"Don't say that to Mom, blasphemer."

Joy smiles.

Dressed and ready, the duo heads downstairs to join the big group of Murphys.

"Oh, look at you two!" Aunt Helen gushes. She reaches for Joy's hand and gives it a squeeze. She has gifts for the girls. Rosaries—lovely white stone rosaries.

"Thank you, Aunt Helen," the two say in unison. They lean in to give their aunt a hug.

"Aren't they nice?" Hannah says. She takes a rosary, has a look, and hands it to Debbie, who smiles.

The girls' little cousin Shaun takes Joy's rosary. He puts the chain around his head like a necklace.

Mrs. Murphy clears her throat, presumably to gently reprimand the boy—too young to know that a rosary is not a necklace—when Shaun puts the crucifix in his mouth, blows and shouts:

"Everybody out of the pool!"

Debbie freezes. For a long second, the entire living room freezes.

Then Hope, Joy, and Hannah erupt in laughter.

Mrs. Murphy and Aunt Helen stare, mortified. They might bless themselves. Debbie, smiling politely, removes the rosary from her son's neck and hands it back to a still giggling Joy.

Debbie clears her throat.

"Should we get to church, then?"

The Murphys and their relatives spill out the front and back doors. Helen will ride with Debbie and her family, allowing Hope, Joy, and Hannah to laugh at their behavior. The sisters trail behind Mr. and Mrs. Murphy out the back door, past the overgrown lilac bush, and through the yard to the station wagon.

"I wonder if that grass is ever going to grow back," Hannah says, pointing toward the large, yellow rectangle where Hank Gehrig used to park his truck.

"The Fabrizios used to have the prettiest yard," Hope says, looking at the yard beyond Gehrigs'.

"Remember when we picked their flowers, and Mr. Fabrizio got so mad?"

"What moron thinks petunias are wildflowers you can pick?" Hannah snorts.

"What were we, four?" Joy asks.

"They really stopped taking care of things after Joannie," Hannah says sadly.

"Keep moving, chickadees," Mr. Murphy says. "Can't be late today."

The clan arrives very early for mass because Hope is a lector, and Bridget is singing.

"Go find Bridget and let her know we're here," Mr. Murphy directs. "I'll let Fr. Bowersox and the Bishop know Hope's ready to read."

"Not fair," Hope grumbles to Joy.

Debbie's son pushes past them and wanders ahead into the large, mostly empty but filling building. Angels circle a dome in the ceiling, virgins and martyrs observe from stained glass windows, and off to the right of the altar, a mournful Christ looks down on his flock from the cross.

Shaun notices the crucifix with horror.

"What happened to that guy?!" he shouts.

Hannah covers her mouth to keep from laughing out loud.

Giggling, Hope and Joy find Bridget exchanging pleasantries with Sheriff Gaietto in the vestibule.

"Surprised to see you here, Sheriff," Bridget offers politely.

"Not exactly my kind of Sunday service," he admits. "I'll be honest, with those robes and the little boys wiping the priests' lips, something smacks of the diabolical in this kind of church."

For the first time, Gaietto had said something that made sense to Hope. Not to Bridget.

"That's disrespectful." Bridget's tone changes. Her back is up. "Why are you here?"

"Just having a little chat with that queer fella upstairs."

"Christopher? Why? What's he done?"

"Just a precaution," Gaietto smirks. He chuckles, nods to the ladies, and leaves the building.

The three sisters mount the winding, wooden staircase to the choir loft, where Bridget will remain during mass to sing. The church organist and Our Lady of Perpetual Help Elementary School music teacher, Christopher Shepard, waits in the choir loft. Short and squat, prematurely balding, Christopher Shepard is fourteen years older than Hope and Joy. They would guess the gap was wider except that he'd gone to high school with Bridget. Wearing a second-hand brown suit, he sits at the grand church organ in his stocking feet and prepares to accompany the girls' oldest sister.

Bridget says hello to Shepard with a wide smile.

"Hello, girls," Christopher Shepard says to Hope and Joy.

"Hey, Shepard," Hope responds flatly.

"Mr. Shepard!" Bridget says to him proudly. "That sounds so grown up and official!"

"I didn't call him Mr. Shepard," Hope corrects with disdain. "Just Shepard. Mister is a sign of respect."

Bridget looks shocked at her sister, who heads with her twin back downstairs to join the rest of the Murphys.

The family, minus Bridget, sits in a pew about 1/3 of the way back from the altar. Other smartly dressed sixth graders pepper the congregation. In a few minutes, each will stand and approach the altar, Fr. Bowersox, and Bishop Franklin to be confirmed.

But first, a reading from the First Letter of Samuel.

Birds flap and squawk in the spring chill, throwing grotesque shadows through the stained glass.

At almost, but not quite, the appointed time, Hope gets up, squeezes past her sisters and cousins, and heads toward the altar, taking her place at the podium. She waits for the pause in the service that lets her know to begin the first reading. The pause doesn't come.

She's gone up too early.

There are still several prayers and at least one song before she can begin the day's readings. She looks confused.

Mass continues.

Hope considers going back to her seat but thinks her time to read will come at any second. Each second seems so long. Is that creepy Howdy Noonan in the front pew?

She looks down at the podium.

She looks back at Fr. Bowersox.

She looks pale.

The room fills with Bridget's voice. She sings "The Lord is Kind and Merciful."

Hope waits for the song to end. Tries to remember what comes next. She feels hot. She looks back down at the page of Samuel. The letters begin to swim.

She looks for Joy.

She looks back at Samuel.

Hope drops to the floor.

She has fainted, her motionless body sprawled behind the podium. The Murphys gasp but don't immediately move.

Bishop Franklin steps over Hope's rag doll body and prepares to read the passage.

Mr. Murphy heads toward the altar to remove his fallen daughter. Hope is long, unruly dead weight, and he has trouble with his grip. An older man from the front pew joins him.

It takes concerted effort, and the older gentleman keeps dropping parts of Hope's lanky frame.

Hannah elbows Joy in the ribs and laughs. Debbie drops her head, her shoulders shaking from her silent laughter.

Joy stares.

The gentlemen finally carry the girl to the vestibule. Mr. Murphy looks back at the family, who try not to draw attention as they stand and head to the back of the church to make their exit.

Mass continues, but technically speaking, Hope and Joy are not confirmed.

Monday before Easter

The following day, Hope stays home from school.

"She's a big faker," Hannah scoffs.

Mrs. Murphy pats Hope's hair.

"Dad will get you to Dr. Mower's later in the morning," she says.

"She's fine," Hannah says.

"Hope so. We'll just check."

"I don't have to stay home with her or anything?" Hannah asks her mother. "I was going to Bernard's."

"No, she'll be fine," she says, still petting Hope's hair. She holds Hope's chin in her hand. "You just stay put."

Everyone gathers their things. Joy and Mr. Murphy walk out the kitchen door, past the crow pecking at the rusted swing set and toward the station wagon out back. Mrs. Murphy moves toward the front door. Because the weather is good, she'll walk up Second Avenue to the end of the street and the ITT office where she's a secretary.

Hannah lingers.

"Maybe clean the bathroom today," she suggests strongly. "And don't eat all the Pringles. I'll come home for lunch, and we can go to Jolly's."

Hope smiles.

She pushes the TV on and looks for Scooby-Doo. She sits on the floor, turning the dial when the front door opens.

The birds in the naked maple make an awful ruckus, and then Eric Stimmell shuts the door behind him. The neighbor on the corner, Eric Stimmell, never knocks, and the Murphys don't lock their doors.

"Oh, hi," he says.

Eric is a big, lumbering man. Hope's never been certain what exactly is wrong with him, just that there is clearly something, and it's the kind of something that leaves Eric Stimmell unacceptable to mock.

There is only one reason a Murphy will forego making fun of another person: pity. You have to be nice to Eric Stimmell.

"Hi," Hope says uncomfortably. "Mom's not home."

"I know," he answers. "She's at work. Saw her walk past the house."

"Oh," Hope responds. "Well, Dad's not home, either. Nobody's home."

"Why are you home?"

"I'm sick."

He walks into the living room and lowers himself awkwardly to the floor. He wears a helmet today—something he's been doing more and more often.

"Is your sister coming home for Easter?"

"Which one? Hannah's home."

"No, Bridget," he smiles. Eric Stimmell is two years older than Bridget and, when she lived at 93 Second, when Hope was very little, he used to walk up and down the back alley hoping to catch her sunbathing.

"Oh," Hope says. "Probably."

She looks around awkwardly. Notices a fresh split on his chin. It's a bad one—looks like a second set of lips.

"Will you get dressed up for Easter?" he asks.

"Just for church."

"Is it your birthday this year?"

"Yep."

"Remember when that kid died on your birthday that time?" he asks.

Hope winces.

"You'll be twelve?" He scooches closer.

"Yep," she repeats, suddenly alarmed.

He leans toward her. It's the kind of move she's only ever seen on TV or in movies, the seductive kiss lean. She reflexively backs away from him. As soon as she's clear of him physically, she stands and bolts upstairs.

Hope runs the length of the hall to her bedroom, shuts the door, which doesn't lock, and perches on the edge of her bed. She moves the country comfort blue rayon curtain her mom just bought from a catalog and peers out the window.

Hope watches, hoping to see Eric Stimmell walk off the front porch and down Second Avenue because what if he doesn't? She has run upstairs, where there is no phone and no exit, she realizes and panics. If she were allowed to watch horror movies, she'd know what to do in this situation, she laments to no one.

She could sneak into her parents' bedroom, climb out the window onto the front porch roof and try to jump to that big, overgrown bush over by Gehrigs' porch. But she would break her leg, and who would help her? Honey Gehrig? One of her boyfriends?

Hope unconsciously fingers the folded corner of a Duran Duran poster, their teased hair barely contained by the bounds of the paper, and peeks back into the front yard. Black birds cackle in the maple by the street.

Hope wishes Hannah would come home.

Hope's eyes fall on an empty Pepsi bottle on the floor next to her bed. She picks it up, turns it over, holds it like a bludgeon, and practices cracking someone's head open with it.

Birds rustle and caw outside her window.

She thinks of a song she hasn't sung in years.

Little bird, little bird

Little beak, little squeak

Fuzzy throat, little peep

Chickadee

Finally, she sees Eric Stimmell lumber down the front porch steps. Hope sighs, the tension releasing from her neck and shoulders. She slides down the slick patchwork bedspread to the floor. She peeks again out the window as he makes his way down the sidewalk past Regina Oliver's house next door, the disturbed birds cawing and flapping in their branches casting a weird shadow behind Eric Stimmell, making it look as if he has wings himself.

He's gone.

Still, she's afraid to go back downstairs.

Hope thinks about cleaning her room, then she thinks about going back to bed. Mostly, she wishes there was a TV and a bathroom upstairs, so she didn't have to go back downstairs.

Then her dad pulls in out front, and she remembers she doesn't have to wait until Hannah decides it's time for Jolly's to go downstairs.

"Let's go see Dr. Mower," her dad calls up from downstairs. "Come on, we're late."

It never occurs to Hope to tell her dad about Eric Stimmell. At lunch, she'll tell Hannah and try to make it a funny story. Because, how dumb is it that Hope didn't just come back down and lock the doors?! She just sat upstairs like an idiot—hilarious! Maybe she'll pantomime Eric leaning toward her for a kiss. Or is that mean?

Hope doesn't like Dr. Mower. He reminds her of Mr. Parkins. He's small, wiry with harshly neat hair and a squirrely way about him. He looks in her ears, up her nose, in her mouth, and lisps that she's healthy.

"Nothing wrong with this one," he says. Dr. Mower talks out of the side of his mouth and spits a bit when he says the letter "s" or "th." Though all Murphy kids do an impression, Hannah's is the best, and Hope is eager to share her diagnosis so Hannah can repeat it in character.

"She's never done that before," Mr. Murphy says. "You don't know why it happened?"

"She's perfectly healthy," Dr. Mower says, shaking his head.

"I guess there's nothing wrong with you that medicine can fix, chickadee," Hope's dad smiles as they head back to the station wagon.

Tuesday before Easter

"Mom wants you to go to Cook's and get some milk," Hannah says.

Hope groans.

"Where's Joy?"

"You don't both have to go everywhere together," Hannah tells her. "Joy's weed-whacking out back before it gets dark."

"I can wait for her."

"If I wanted you to wait for her, I'd have you out back helping her. Go to the store, ya lazy cow."

Hope cuts through Regina Oliver's yard then crosses the street to avoid walking directly in front of Eric Stimmell's house. She crosses back a few houses past.

It's already getting dark.

Nothing sits in the lot outside Cook's besides a beat-up white pick-up.

The harshly lit little store is empty except for the buzz of the fluorescents and the middle-aged woman at the register. Bucky the deer head hangs just this side of the register, low enough for Odenton kids to pet. Hope never, ever pets Bucky. She lingers at the tiny magazine stand to see if there's a new Star Hits magazine. She longs for unseen pictures of Duran Duran, but the only Star Hits is the same one she perused on her last trip to Cook's when Katrina McCoy pocketed a Three Musketeers.

Disappointed, Hope grabs a gallon of milk, hoists it to the register belt, pays the bored cashier, and leaves.

Back in the parking lot, it seems much darker already. The milk is heavy and sweaty. Hope wants to set it on the ground and run back inside.

Why is it so dark?

Hope holds the cold gallon against her hip and starts through the parking lot. Better to cross the street now than to wait until she's closer to Stimmells'.

The houses of Second Avenue flank the street, aging and menacing. There's not a soul outside except Hope. She decides to just walk straight down the middle of the road, safe in the glow of the streetlamps.

There is no sound.

The milk is cold, wet, and heavy against her hip.

Suddenly a rush of flapping draws her eye toward the Stimmell barn, still six or seven houses ahead.

She starts mindlessly singing.

Forever more and ever more
Beneath the bush, behind the door
Fuzzy throat, little peep
Secret place, you and me
Chick, chick, chick, chick, chickadee

As she walks, she watches her shadow, a great grey blob with a gallon-sized lump around its hip. Her shadow gets bigger and bigger until it takes up nearly the whole spotlight. It seems to take on a new shape…one with wings.

She stops singing and listens, but she doesn't turn around. A distant clicking sound, then car wheels on gravel.

She steps out of the spotlight and into the dark street. She quickens her pace.

Staring directly ahead to the next spotlight on the blacktop from the lamp overhead, she tells herself it's nothing. It's nothing.

She sings.

She does a little hop step.

The clicking gets louder. She turns to see the white pick-up bearing down on her, its headlights dark. She stumbles out of the way. It turns down the street before Regina Oliver's house and disappears beyond the Stimmells' barn.

Hope collects herself, then she notices Eric Stimmell on his porch.

He waves.

She freezes.

She hears a distant click.

Eric lumbers toward her.

She stares. She doesn't move.

The clicking gets louder. Closer.

Eric bounds toward Second Ave.

Hope can see the truck out of the corner of her eye.

"Stop!"

She screams it. She doesn't decide to do it; she just blurts it and realizes she's yelling as she hears herself do it.

Startled, Eric Stimmell stops moving.

The truck speeds between them, Hope hugs the wet gallon to her chest and runs home.

Wednesday before Easter

Hope, Joy and Isabel walk down Sandusky Street, away from their squat elementary school, toward home.

"Easter break, bitches!" Isabel cheers. "How much you got, picky eater?"

"Short week," Joy worries. "May not be enough."

Hope looks at the lunch money she has not spent on lunch and counts.

"You're probably hungry," Isabel says. "I would starve."

"She's always like that," Joy says. "She spends half her life alone at the kitchen table staring at cold food she won't eat."

"Why stare at it?" Isabel asks.

"They won't let me leave until I eat. So, when I don't eat, I just sit there until they give up."

"Willful," Joy says.

"Not a good daughter, like Joy," Isabel smiles wickedly.

Hope's still counting.

"Let's figure it out at McCarten's," Isabel recommends. "See how many Tootsie Rolls and Jolly Ranchers you can afford."

"I don't even like Jolly Ranchers."

The candy is at the counter just inside the door. Mrs. McCarten, thin with bangs and a puffy-sleeved shirt, stands there, as always. They've never seen her anywhere but behind that counter in the front corner of what would be called a country store if it were anywhere but the second-largest street in Odenton.

The girls have never been beyond that counter, never ventured into the aisles to investigate McCarten wares, never looked around to find what lay in the back of the store.

Hope pulls a bill and some coins from the front pocket of her polyester blend pants, and Isabel starts counting out Tootsie Rolls and Jolly Ranchers. Hope spies caramel crèmes and redirects her.

"Caramel crèmes," she says, pointing to the clear plastic tub.

"Please?"

"No," Joy decides, taking the Jolly Ranchers from the counter in front of Isabel and dropping them back into their beer-barrel style holder.

"Hey, remember root beer barrels?" Joy asks.

"Yeah, they were good," Isabel says. "Tasted like root beer."

"Aunt Helen always had a little bowl full of them," Hope says, still counting Tootsie Rolls. "And butterscotches."

"I hate butterscotch," Isabel says.

Hope and Joy stare at her and gasp.

"Well, hello ladies," a high, whining voice behind them opens a conversation.

"Hey, Shepard," Hope says, diverting her attention from the growing piles for only a second.

He leans in over the sixth graders' shoulders. He smells like Old Spice. The girls duck slightly to avoid contact, Hope scooping candy toward her as she does.

"I can help you right over here," Mrs. McCarten smiles at him suspiciously.

"What have you got there?" he asks the girls. He ignores Mrs. McCarten outright.

Hope looks back.

"Are you growing a mustache?" Isabel asks.

"I've had a mustache for years," he claims. "You like it?"

Isabel shrugs.

"I agree with you sisters," he says, sidling up toward Isabel. "I think butterscotch candies are delicious."

Something about the way he sing-songs the word 'delicious' makes Hope sneer.

"But those caramels are even better," he says, leaning into Joy and pointing. His hand is hairy, like the twins' dad's, and a few greys wind around his cheap watch.

"Girls, can you move your piles to the side a bit, so I have room to check out this customer?" Mrs. McCarten asks.

"Oh, I'll wait," Shepard says, still smiling at Isabel.

"We'll just take these, then," Joy decides, pushing the piles toward Mrs. McCarten.

"I wonder how your dad would feel about you gorging on all this candy," Shepard says to the Murphy girls. "I won't tell if you give me a piece."

He turns his strange smile to the sisters.

Mrs. McCarten scoops all the candies into a small paper bag, hands them to Hope, and says, "Go home now."

The three push past Shepard. The little bell against the door chimes as they tumble through it onto the sidewalk and toward home. Once outside, the three look at each other, burst out laughing, and begin running for Sandusky Bridge.

By the time they hit the bridge, their bag of snacks is much depleted. They stop, lean on the fat metal railing and float Tootsie Roll wrappers in the breeze toward the train tracks below.

"He's so creepy," Isabel says.

"And that mustache," Joy says. "Like he's Magnum."

"Mini-Magnum," Isabel says.

"He probably sits alone up in the choir loft admiring it," Hope says, pantomiming a sinister mustache twirl with her fingers.

Isabel digs into the bag. "But hey, free candy!"

"What's happening down there?" Hope points to an enormous flock of squawking black birds hovering around the yard of a dilapidated house. The backyard runs right up against the tracks. The birds dodge and dive around the roofs of nearby homes. Just beyond those roofs, you can make out the metal ice cream swirl of Coney Castle.

"Where did they come from?" Isabel asks.

"There are so many!" Hope points to birds in trees, on a clothesline, in bunches on the tracks, and in the yard. "I'd be afraid to go in that yard."

"They could come up here," Isabel says.

"Why, yes," Joy replies drily. "They can fly."

Later in the evening, Hope and Joy have quizzed each other on their spelling words. Hope struggled through the math homework Joy had finished in minutes, and both were now quietly lounging on the beige, flowered couch their mom picked out not long after Hannah left for college.

Mr. and Mrs. Murphy are out buying groceries.

The twins and their Aunt Helen are watching WKRP in Cincinnati, which makes Hope feel very adult.

"I hope Hannah brings home ice cream," Hope announces wistfully to the room.

"Me, too," Aunt Helen says with a giggle.

Hope and Joy laugh.

"He's pretty cute, that one," Helen says of the show's tight panted program director, Andy Travis. Hope and Joy like the character Dr. Johnny Fever, but wish he was cuter so they could like him more. This may be the first TV show the girls liked that did not involve a crush of any kind.

"I like his dimples," Helen says.

Hannah bursts in the kitchen door, startling the three in the living room. She bounds heavy-footed and panicked through the kitchen toward her family.

Joy and Hope are alarmed. This is not the natural Hannah. Her demeanor is marked usually by disdain followed by a bit of mockery and then a task.

"I hate to put all those small animals out of a home, Hope, but go wash your hair."

That kind of thing.

"Hannah, what is it?" Helen asks her.

"Somebody jumped me!"

"What?!!" the three respond in unison.

"In the alley behind Coney Castle. I was walking home, and somebody jumped on my back!"

"Oh my God!" her aunt says. She stands, the blue crocheted blanket sliding from her skinny legs. She reaches toward her niece and then covers her mouth with her hands.

"He was pretty small, so I threw him off and ran home!"

Hannah pantomimes this—falling forward a little as an invisible someone leaps onto her back, then reaching behind her, grabbing and throwing.

Hope and Joy stare with bewilderment.

Then they laugh.

Helen seems startled.

Hannah looks at her family with wounded surprise for a minute, then she laughs, herself.

"Who would jump somebody bigger than them?" Joy laughs. She mimics Hannah's pantomime.

Helen finally laughs.

Hope laughs until she's red-faced.

"It was probably a McCoy boy," Hannah says.

"Are you sure, Hannah?" Helen asks. "Did you see him?"

"No."

"You just threw him to the ground?" Hope asks.

Hannah laughs a little but gets excited again.

"He just jumped on my back," she pantomimes, hunching over a little as if some small load had just dropped onto her back. She claws at her imaginary assailant, pulls him off, and jogs toward her sisters.

They all laugh again—the image is too hilarious.

Until Mr. and Mrs. Murphy come home.

Thirty minutes or so after the incident, Hannah has showered, Helen is picking up a crossword her sister didn't finish, and Joy and Hope are fighting against going to bed. Mr. and Mrs. Murphy come in the front door.

"Groceries in the car," Mr. Murphy announces. "Everybody grab a bag."

"Somebody jumped on Hannah's back when she was walking home from Coney Castle!" Hope declares.

The tenor seems different now, though. Mr. and Mrs. Murphy's faces drop.

"What?" James Murphy says, staring at his daughter for answers.

Hannah shrugs it off.

"Oh, it wasn't such a much."

"No, it was really funny!" Hope informs him. "She was walking home, and a McCoy boy jumped on her back, but he was little, and she is big, and she tossed him off her back and ran home!"

Mr. Murphy runs his big hand over his face.

"Did anyone call the police?" Mrs. Murphy asks.

"Oh, Mom," Hannah dismisses them. "No one was hurt. What does it matter?"

Nearly two hours later, Mrs. Murphy is still unconvinced, but she is sorry she decided to make the call to Sheriff Gaietto.

"And I thought Bridget was the pretty Murphy girl!" the sheriff says, sizing up Hannah.

Joy rolls her eyes.

Hannah grits her teeth.

Gaietto asks about a cup of coffee and listens over his shoulder as Hannah recounts the story. He wanders with interest from room to room, opening closet doors, peering up the stairs toward the bedrooms.

Mr. Murphy hands him his cup of coffee.

"Do you need us to come down to the station or look at mugshots or something?" he asks.

Gaietto laughs.

"Best idea is just to keep your daughter away from dark alleys if you want my expert opinion."

"Too much to hope you could just keep the town safe, I guess," Mrs. Murphy responds flatly.

Gaietto throws her a surprised look. He straightens himself to face her directly and looks her in the eye.

She looks back.

"Hannah, who did you say it might be?" Helen asks, trying to break the tension as much as help.

"A McCoy boy," Hope speaks up.

The sheriff walks toward the ganglier of the twins.

"You had a spill at church recently, isn't that right?" he asks her, but his voice doesn't sound sympathetic. Hope doesn't answer—the word "spill" confuses her slightly, and his tone scares her.

"I don't know if it was a McCoy," Hannah admits.

Gaietto huffs.

"Well, they are rowdy boys."

He thinks about it, turns his attention to Hannah.

"Are you saying you think they might be involved in the dark arts?"

Hannah laughs out loud.

"No one said anything about dark arts," Mrs. Murphy corrects him.

"Literally, no one in this house has ever used the phrase 'dark arts,'" Hannah laughs.

Gaietto shakes his head at their naivete.

"The one who does what is sinful is of the devil," Gaietto tells her. "Book of John. You never know what you'll find in the dark around this town," he says eerily. "Could be someone looking for a young virgin."

He winks at Hannah, who shudders visibly.

"Do you ever solve a crime?" she asks him bluntly.

"Isn't it usually the most obvious person?" Aunt Helen asks, somewhat desperate to get the conversation back on track.

Gaietto shakes his head and chuckles. He looks amiably at Helen.

"Not in this town. Not in my experience."

He clears his throat dramatically, nods at Mrs. Murphy, and takes a long drink from his coffee.

"The way you do things," Mrs. Murphy walks toward him. "Blaming ghouls—it doesn't help anything. It's all boogeymen. What you do just invites evil."

Gaietto sets his cup on the coffee table. Hannah covertly slides a coaster under it.

"You should be a better example to these girls," he tells her. "And learn to hold your tongue."

Mrs. Murphy is done.

"Get out of my house."

Holy Thursday

"Hannah, you don't want to come to see Hope and Joy's little play?" Mrs. Murphy asks.

"I will pass. I'll clean the house." She looks at her sisters. "And then you guys can keep things clean while everybody's here this weekend."

She eyes the girls with authority and pre-emptive disappointment.

"We'll be there almost every night this week for Holy Week—I don't know why they couldn't skip the PTO this month," Mr. Murphy complains.

"Hon," his wife gives him the stink eye. "Remember, Hope's skit is today for the meeting."

"It's a play," Hope corrects.

"Oh, is it?" her dad smiles and pulls her in for a squeeze. She smiles, but the zipper on his jacket is cold and jagged against her face.

"It is," Joy confirms.

In the basement meeting room of the elementary school, Joy, Hope, and several other twelve-year-olds gather to perform.

Howdy Noonan, a tall, sturdy boy from the high school, looks uncomfortable in his dress shoes as he reads from the New Testament to begin the meeting.

Mr. and Mrs. Murphy sit among the parents, teachers, and staff, facing the cleared floor space beneath the massive crucifix on the front wall.

Mrs. Marinis addresses the group.

"Before we begin, we have another student-written and performed skit for you," she announces. "This month, our 6th graders will perform—"

She leans toward Hope.

"What's the skit called?" she whispers.

"*When a Stranger Calls.*"

Joy, playing the lead role of a babysitter, sits on a beanbag chair in front of a cardboard box made to look like a console TV. Three small-for-their-ages sixth-graders sit on the floor in front of her. They all look toward the box. Inside that box, a freckle-faced redhead looks out the custom-made TV screen toward her classmates and the audience beyond.

"Flash, Norman Criminal has just escaped," she announces, TV-newscaster-like, stumbling over the word "criminal." Off to the side, Hope curses herself for not naming the killer Norman Crook.

"Lock your doors and windows. He kills!"

"Time for bed, kids," Joy says to her charges on the floor.

The three kids exit "stage" left. Joy returns to the beanbag chair. Offstage, an unreasonably sweaty sixth-grade boy called Mickey Wright yells, "ring, ring!"

Joy answers the blue plastic toy phone on the prop end table.

Again, from offstage, Mickey Wright yells: "Have you checked the children?"

Parents in the audience start to get antsy. Many smile weirdly and look around at each other.

Joy hangs up and dials the authorities.

Hope knocks at the pretend door.

"I'm officer Murphy," she says. "You're having trouble with your phone?"

Parents laugh.

Hope picks up the phone. She looks dramatically at the crowd, then back to her sister.

"The calls are coming from inside the house," she announces.

The girls' classmate jumps out from behind the cardboard box TV, where he's been squatting the entire performance. He stabs Officer Murphy, who dies with a flourish on the floor.

"No one can help you!" he yells, more to the crowd than to Joy. "I killed the kids when I was upstairs. I killed the mom and dad when they left for dinner. And now, I'll kill you!"

The killer jumps at Joy, stabs her, she dies on the floor with a bit more understatement, and he runs to the front door. He pauses to look at the carnage behind him, looks to an entirely silent crowd, and says, "I wonder who's home next door?"

THE END

Maureen Murphy covers her face with her hands. James Murphy puts one arm around her, shaking his head.

No one claps.

Howdy Noonan, now sitting alone in a folding chair in the back row, laughs out loud.

Back at 93 Second, Mr. and Mrs. Murphy aren't really speaking to the girls.

"Well, my lord, it's just a silly play," Mrs. Murphy explains to Bridget on the phone.

"What did you do?!" Hannah says in mock surprise to Hope. "You little weirdo."

"She doesn't need counseling," their mother announces into the receiver. "Honestly, if it weren't for all this hoopla the sheriff dredges up, we could just call this another one of the girls' little quirks."

"So, it didn't go well?" Hannah surmises when her mother hangs up the phone.

Mrs. Murphy sighs.

"You'll need to stop writing for a while, Hope," She delivers the line with tempered compassion. "And there are some kids you're supposed to steer clear of for a bit."

"Good going, psycho," Hannah laughs. "What did she do?"

Their mother sighs again.

"Her skit was based on a movie about— I don't know—murdering children, I guess."

Hannah looks at Hope and Joy in surprise.

"*When a Stranger Calls*," Joy clarifies.

Hannah erupts in laughter.

"Oh my God!" she chokes out. "Well, that is just priceless."

"OLPH faculty did not find it priceless," Mrs. Murphy responds flatly.

"Oh, they should just settle down. What harm is it? Some kids saw a commercial for a movie and wrote about it—who cares?" She laughs again, then stops. "Where was their teacher for all this? I mean, why didn't she stop them?"

"That's a good question," Mrs. Murphy realizes, looking to the twins for an answer.

"She had us rehearse during recess," Hope says.

"She didn't watch," Joy confirms.

"That fine Catholic education in action," Hannah smirks.

Good Friday

"Just let them go," Hannah counsels. "It's a birthday party. What's the worst that could happen? They'll eat pepperoni?"

Dad shakes his head.

"Maybe if they're seen as a little more reverent than those others, people will stop calling them creepy."

"That is the opposite of what will happen," Hannah tells him. "Please believe me."

While they argue, Joy and Hope sneak out the back door.

They walk to Isabel's house, and the three sit, as they often do, on the front porch – away from Isabel's three brothers. The girls wear light jackets, but the sun is bright, and spring feels like it's trying to be born.

"Are you going to Michelle's birthday party?" Hope asks.

"My mom won't let me," Isabel says. "She says it's not right to celebrate on Good Friday."

"That's what Dad says, but Hannah says it's a cheap way to piggyback birthday parties," Joy explains.

"They never throw you a birthday party."

"We'll just pretend Michelle's party is for us, too," Hope decides. "If they let us go."

"If the party was for you, my mom might let me go," Isabel says.

"She's not mad about my play?" Hope asks. She almost doesn't ask because she doesn't really want to know.

"Mom and Dad didn't go to PTO last night. She just doesn't want me to go over to Michelle's. Their whole family's kind of wrong in the head." Isabel considers. "It must suck to have a birthday that comes on a holiday."

"It doesn't always," Hope corrects her.

The screen door from the next porch over slams. Ray Ray, the old man who lives there, takes his seat on his metal glider. He's almost entirely bald and almost entirely skinny except for an enormous belly that makes it tough for his pants to figure out how to stay put.

"Ray Ray!" Isabel shouts. "Hey, Ray Ray! Are you going to Michelle's birthday party?"

He responds with indecipherable grunts, then spits, and the three girls break into peals of laughter.

"He's Michelle's grampa?" Joy whispers.

Ray Ray grins at Joy, spits, and unleashes another string of utterly unintelligible sounds.

The three laugh again but grow restless.

"Let's see if we have enough pop bottles to buy anything at Cook's," Isabel suggests.

They hop off the porch, wave at Ray Ray, and disappear through a side door. The trio grabs returnable Pepsi bottles from the dusty stairs leading to the basement. Hope pauses, staring a long while into the darkness at the bottom of the steps.

"Bzz bzz bzz – Hey bumblebee!" Isabel calls to her.

Hope snaps out of it, grabs a carrier, and follows her friend and sister back into the alley.

Michelle's mother emerges from Ray Ray's front door as they leave. She looks like the male singer from a 70s rock band, all ribcage and tight jeans, tank top, and greasy brown hair.

"Hey girls!" she says, noticing the three and their pop bottles. "See you tonight?"

The three wave and begin the trek to Cook's.

Once inside, Isabel pets Bucky's nose and sets her bottles at the register. The girls follow, and the three wait for their money.

"Big bag of Bugles and more pop," Isabel decides.

"Candy," Hope counters.

"Salty," Joy says. "Salty is better with pop."

"I like candy and pop," Hope whines.

Isabel elbows Joy and nonchalantly points. Over near the magazines, it's Shepard.

"He's like a grocery store ghost," Isabel whispers. "He haunts us."

Shepard turns toward the girls and smiles slyly. Hope backs into Bucky.

"More treats, girls?" Shepard asks. "Aren't you worried about your figures?"

Joy winces.

The freezer beyond Bucky sputters loudly. Hope looks past the deer head to see water begin to roll out from under the freezer, pooling in every direction. She watches it slowly spread under the deer head, its dead eye level with hers. She wants to hang her jacket on its antlers to hide its face.

"So, what are we snacking on today, young ladies?"

Isabel and Joy look at each other and smirk. The woman behind the counter notes the water and leaves the situation behind her, searching for a mop.

Shepard takes a step toward Joy.

"Do you need some help deciding?"

Hope looks from the antler to Shepard, her feet wet. Shepard steps on the slick floor and slides just slightly. He is just beyond Hope's grip.

He takes another step, his cheap loafers slipping again in the wet. Bucky stares blankly at Shepard, his antlers casting a pointy shadow that stabs at Shepard's body.

Hope stares.

Isabel looks at the cash in her hand. She sighs, grabs Joy by the elbow, nudges Hope, and the three leave the store empty-handed.

"Where you going, girls?" Shepard calls behind them.

Out in the parking lot, Isabel kicks at the gravel.

"Free candy last time, no candy this time."

The girls sigh. Walking back, they pass 93 Second. Hannah sits on the front porch.

"Hey skags, get inside to eat before your party," she says.

Joy and Hope perk up at the news.

"We can go?" Hope asks.

Hannah nods.

"We'll eat there," Joy says.

"Dad's afraid they'll feed you meat."

"They're Catholic," Hope tells her.

"Yeah, the kind of Catholic that throws a party on Good Friday."

"Heathens," Isabel whispers, then giggles. She waves at the sisters and walks on as the girls go inside for battered fish and au gratin potatoes from a box.

By nine that night, four little girls – none of them Isabel - snuggle into sleeping bags on the worn yellow and brown of Michelle Kirschner's living room carpet. Michelle's mom drinks more than she should, and the family has Cinemax, which is where things begin to go awry.

All facing the TV from between couches and chairs, girls snack on Doritos and Bugles, drink Pepsi from 2-litres and watch whatever happens to be playing on Cinemax.

On an average day, Hope and Joy are lucky to convince their parents to allow PG-rated movies, so unfettered access to cable viewing is a heady, dangerous treat for them.

The birthday girl peruses her cable guide. Michelle Kirschner is skinny and blond, very small for her age. She shoos her little brother in his Knight Rider pj's out of the room.

"The first one is called Happy Hooker Goes to Hollywood," she grins.

Youngsters twitter and hide their faces. Hope and Joy look at each other, maybe worried.

The film is a little more than halfway over when the girls turn it on.

"Wait until your mom goes to bed," Molly Gross—whose own mother had made the twins their glorious peasant skirts for Confirmation—whispers.

"She won't care," Michelle counters. "Besides, it will be over by then."

Adam West, whom most of the kids know from Batman reruns, co-stars. With its four-p.m. timeslot and double bill with the iconic Seventies Wonder Woman program, Batman is pretty typical post-school day viewing. But the girls have never seen Batman behave like this.

Molly and Michelle poke each other and giggle. Hope oscillates between looking, blushing, and shielding her eyes.

Joy's attention is fixed on the smoky kitchen where Mrs. Kirschner quietly argues on the phone.

Joy stands up, stays close to the wall, and creeps toward the kitchen. Though most of the girls are distracted by their first nude scene, Hope watches Joy instead. Joy edges to the wooden archway between the living room soft-core-porn party and the kitchen. She fingers some dried jelly on the wooden doorway frame as she draws her ear to the edge of the room.

Hope holds her breath.

"God damn it!" they hear, and Mrs. Kirschner slams the phone. Joy hops back to the floor next to her sister.

"Who's she talking to?" Hope whispers.

"Mr. Kirschner, I think."

"Then who's that man in the kitchen?" Hope wonders.

Joy doesn't answer.

"What man?" Molly whispers. The youngsters sneak over and cluster close together as the tension from the kitchen starts to penetrate the mood.

"The one in the corner," Hope says. Molly strains her head to see into the kitchen from the dark living room floor.

"There's nobody there," she says.

"There's no man here," Michelle clarifies. "Just my little brother."

"Your mom sounds really mad," Molly worries. "Will she be mad if she sees what we're watching?"

"She's just mad at my dad," Michelle responds without emotion. "We'll be fine. It's over anyway."

"What's on next?" Molly asks eagerly.

"Motel Hell!" Michelle answers.

Joy and Hope exchange another worried glance. Their first horror movie.

Each slumber party attendee pretends to be brave as they watch a car pop tires on barbed wire strung across an unlit country road. A young woman wakes up in a farmhouse with a kindly farmer and his portly sister looking on.

The girls yawn. Some start to doze.

"This is boring," Molly complains.

"No, wait!" Michelle commands. "I know it will get better. It's rated R!"

Sounds of a chainsaw. Gurgling noises from sacks placed over something planted behind the barn.

Now, the girls are awake. Awake and fidgeting.

Hope escapes into the bathroom.

Michelle's guinea pig sits in a converted fish tank on the floor near a towel rack in the little room cramped with hampers and store-bought shelving. Since she doesn't have to go, Hope leans against the sink and stares at the beast. She covers her ears with her hands.

Joy knocks. She comes in; they close the door and look at the animal.

"I don't want to go back out there," Hope says.

"You are afraid of everything."

"I wish Isabel was here."

"They'd still have that movie on," Joy reminds her.

"I wish we'd stayed home."

"It's almost our birthday, so it's almost like our birthday party," Joy says. "We should try to have fun."

"But that little pig sounds just like those headbags." Hope tries not to whine.

"We're going back," Joy says firmly.

A knock interrupts them. It's Michelle.

"Hey, I need to pee."

Back in the living room, Molly asks, "Do you want to turn this off?"

Hope looks at Joy. Neither answer.

Michelle returns from the bathroom, looks accusingly at Molly. "Are you a baby?"

"No. It's just dumb."

The screen door off the kitchen slams. Birds outside caw and cackle at the noise.

Mr. Kirschner is home. He stands in the doorway between the darkened kitchen and the living room, lit only by the horrific images on the console TV.

"Hello, birthday girl," he says smiling, just the hint of a slur.

"Hi, Dad," Michelle says without looking away from the TV.

Mr. Kirschner stands in the doorway a minute longer. Hope thinks he looks sad.

"Where the fuck have you been?!" an unseen Mrs. Kirschner stage-whispers from behind him. He turns and disappears into the kitchen.

By the end of the movie, the girls have worked their way to within a few inches of each other, huddling together in the glow of the television, leaning away from the kitchen. They finish the movie, ignoring as best they can the sounds of Michelle's drunken parents exchanging words.

As Michelle flips through the cable guide, Molly pulls her Strawberry Shortcake sleeping bag up to her chin, closes her eyes, and wills herself to sleep.

"This is why Isabel wasn't allowed to come," Joy says to her sister.

"Naked TV or foul-mouthed parent-fighting?"

"Yes."

Michelle is still watching TV, but Joy and Hope decide to follow Molly's lead.

Sometime later, Hope is thirsty. She tiptoes into the kitchen. The floor reflects the moon so brightly she has to shield her eyes. The light inside the fridge is even brighter. All she can see is the vibrant red of the Kool-Aid. She stares at it, then slams the refrigerator door. She looks at the picture of Michelle under a magnet on the fridge. She's dressed for confirmation, her hands folded proudly in front of her.

"What's up, kiddo?" she hears.

On her left, Mr. Parkins sits in the Kirschner breakfast nook, fork and knife in hand, a paper napkin tucked into the neck of his bloody undershirt, a fish flopping on the plate in front of him.

Hope stares.

"You're the devil," she hears from behind her somewhere. She peers around and looks into the darkness.

It's not yet light when Molly pokes Hope.

Red and blue light swirls through the dark living room.

"We're supposed to call home now," Molly says.

Hope stays still.

"No breakfast or anything!" Molly whispers with shock and disappointment. "You guys should stay over at my house next time. We have HBO."

Hope shakes her sister and feels under the pillow for her glasses.

"We're supposed to call home," Molly repeats.

An older woman Hope doesn't know kneels down on the floor among the girls. Joy sits up.

"It's time to go, girls," she says. "Quickly now, let's all walk into the kitchen, and you can call your parents."

"It's dark out," Molly complains. "My mom will be sleeping."

"I know, doll," the woman says firmly but kindly. "You'll need to wake her."

Sleepy little girls stand in a line at the wall phone in the kitchen. Sheriff Gaietto watches from the darkened doorway.

The Murphy phone rings and rings.

"Just let it ring, sweetheart," the woman tells Joy. She walks toward the front door and Sheriff Gaietto. The lights shining on her remind Hope of Christmas.

The lady waves. Hope leans forward to see into the yard. Michelle and her brother, in his Knight Rider pajamas, get into a car with another older woman. They all wave back at the woman in the doorway. She looks sad and tired – like Mr. Kirschner.

Hannah answers.

"They want us to come home," Joy tells her.

From where she stands next to Joy, Hope can hear Hannah.

"What?! What did you do?"

"I don't know," Joy answers.

"Mom and Dad are asleep."

"They really want us to go," Joy tells her. "Can you come?"

Holy Saturday

"Hope and Joy," Hannah loud-whispers to wake them. "Wake up. You slept too late. Dad took Mom to the hospital this morning."

The girls sit up.

"She was feeling poorly, having trouble breathing," she says. "Aunt Helen went with them. That was a while ago. You should get up. We'll get the house clean, so it looks nice when they get back."

Joy stands. Hope climbs down from the top bunk.

Hannah pulls a straggling hair tie from Joy's hair and re-ties her ponytail.

"Mom's in the hospital?"

"They had to go to the Emergency Room because it's Saturday," Hannah explains. "Dr. Mower wasn't in, so that's what they had to do. I don't think they'll admit her or anything."

Still wearing their Muppet pajamas, the girls walk silently to the kitchen, toast Pop-Tarts, clean their dishes and turn to Hannah.

"Joy gets the bathroom," she says. "You put on some shoes and sweep the porch and front sidewalk."

The girls comply. Out front, Hope wishes she'd put on some clothes and a jacket, too. Her green Kermit pajama pants are far too short, her skinny, white ankles exposed and cold.

She moves two plastic chairs to one side of the porch and begins sweeping. As she gets to the black wrought iron on the Honey Gehrig side of the porch, she notices the birds.

She hadn't looked up before now, and they hadn't made a noise. But there are so many in that bush overtaking the Gehrig porch that it looks like some freakish, overly decorated Christmas tree. She backs toward the unswept side of her own porch, turning her gaze to the street where blackbirds crowd the maples.

They're all silent, and they all seem to be facing Hope. She backs toward her front door and slips inside.

"Done?" Hannah asks suspiciously.

"I'm cold."

Hannah rolls her eyes.

"It's cold out!" Hope yells. She pushes past Hannah and stalks toward the stairs to the second floor.

"Oh, ya big baby," Hannah calls after her. "I'll finish the porch. Go make Mom and Dad's bed."

Hope doesn't say anything, but she sneaks over toward her dad's cluttered, never-used desk and tries to peek through the window that looks out over the porch. She sees Hannah's back, the broom in her hand, her head down. If Hannah notices the birds, she doesn't let on.

Hope goes upstairs, dresses, and makes her parents' bed.

Later, the girls are done with their chores, and all three sisters sit, fidgety and impatient in the living room. Finally, Aunt Helen and the Murphy parents return, Mr. Murphy carrying a bag of donuts he picked up from the bakeshop across from Mercy Hospital.

"Oh, doesn't the house look sparkling clean, Maureen?" Aunt Helen asks her sister.

"It does," Mrs. Murphy says weakly, and then with more energy, "Thank you, Hannah! Thank you, girls. Dad has donuts."

Mrs. Murphy lowers herself into her rocker. Mr. Murphy hands the bag to Hannah and pulls the blue, crocheted afghan from the back of the couch, draping it over his wife's legs. She squeezes his hand.

"Save one for me, chickadees!" he says, turning back to the bag.

Hope grabs something, pleased to find a cruller in her hands, although Joy's traditional glazed looks really good.

Aunt Helen gets comfortable on the beige couch that still looks pretty new.

"Tell us about your slumber party, girls," she says. "Did you have fun?"

Hannah laughs out loud.

"Yes," the girls say in unison, and then nothing more.

"Do you want me to put some music on?" Hannah asks her mom.

"That would be lovely."

"And can you fix me a cup?" Mr. Murphy asks, settling into the big blue chair across from his wife.

Hannah shoots Hope and Joy a look, and they head to the kitchen to make some instant coffee.

"Anybody else?" Joy asks.

"Tea, please?" Helen requests.

Hours later, the girls have been listless most of the day—not enough sleep, although no one brings up the slumber party again. No one talks about much, actually.

The Love Boat is on. Hope and Joy sit on the couch on either side of their dad. Their mom sits in her rocking chair and sips port wine from a jelly glass. Aunt Helen, a jelly glass of port wine in her hand as well, sits on the edge of the big blue chair nearest Mom's rocker—the chair Mr. Murphy usually uses.

No one has said anything about Mrs. Murphy's trip to the hospital besides, "Oh, it's nothing."

Hannah's heading out to see her boyfriend, Bernard.

"Classy, Mom," she points at the glass.

"If the glass is good enough for my orange juice, it's good enough," Mrs. Murphy says.

Hannah laughs and opens the front door

"Hope and Joy," she hollers behind her. "There's a bunch of skags on the front porch for you."

Isabel pokes her head in and waves.

"Hello, sweetheart," Mrs. Murphy waves.

Hope and Joy move toward the front porch.

Isabel is out there with Katrina McCoy – short, athletic, smiley – and Mickey Wright. A boy. How odd.

Joy closes the door.

"What happened last night?!" Katrina bursts.

"What happened?" Hope asks.

"Oh my God," Isabel says. "You were there, right? Michelle Kirschner's mom shot her dad!"

"What?!" Hope is stunned. She looks at Joy, who shrugs.

"Didn't you stay over?" Isabel asks.

"Yeah, but we didn't see that or anything," Hope offers.

"And you didn't hear anything today?" Katrina accuses in disbelief.

"Our mom—" Hope begins.

"We had to clean the house," Joy interrupts her.

"Some lady woke us up in the middle of the night to go home, though," Hope remembers. "That must have been why."

"So crazy," Mickey Wright, a boy, says.

"Let's take off," Katrina suggests, making faces to suggest they have more to say than can safely be shared on the Murphy porch.

Hope opens the door a crack.

"Mom, can we—?"

Her dad answers.

"No."

"Oh, hon," Mrs. Murphy responds.

"With God-knows-who out there on the loose?"

"We do know who, and she's hardly on the loose now, is she?" Mrs. Murphy returns. "Go ahead, girls. Don't be out too late."

Hope looks at Joy as she closes the door.

"I think she already knew about Michelle's mom."

"Everybody knows!" Katrina shouts.

Aunt Helen opens the door, smiling. The children freeze.

She walks out the door gingerly, stooped to one side, and wearing a housedress. Hope and Joy think nothing of this because Aunt Helen is always wearing a housedress by this time of day, though it occurs to Hope just now that she's never seen anyone else wear one.

Helen's wearing slippers and she looks cold.

"Brrrr," she smiles at the kids. "Hullo – I'm the girls' auntie visiting from Pennsylvania."

Joy and Hope's friends smile politely.

"We've had some big excitement around here today," she says with an animated delivery. "Girls, don't be out too late, OK? Your dad's been through a lot today."

Hope and Joy nod.

The group walks down Second Avenue, seemingly aimless. Isabel turns to Mickey Wright and appears to pick up a conversation they may have been having before Hope and Joy joined the group.

"You shouldn't smoke pot, though," she says. "It's really bad for you."

"I don't know," he murmurs.

"No, it's really bad. You shouldn't do it," Isabel argues. "Right, Hope?"

"I think it's better than real cigarettes, though, right?" Hope wonders.

Isabel looks angry. Mickey smiles. The group keeps walking.

"I cannot believe Mrs. Kirschner shot Mr. Kirschner," Hope says.
"What does Ray Ray think?" Mickey asks.

"Ray Ray thinks it's funny!" Isabel says. "He has no idea what got into her last night, but he says that man's been asking for it for years. He's calling her Sure Shot Kirschner."

"Oh, that is awesome," Mickey admires.

"Shurshy for short," Joy jokes.

"Even better," Mickey decides.

"Except Mr. Kirschner lived, right? So, she's not that sure a shot," Joy notes.

"Still, a great nickname," Mickey points out.

Eventually, Joy asks: "Where are we going?"

"Not much farther," Katrina says.

In fact, they walk all the way past OLPH elementary school, and then Katrina steers the group into a trailer park eyeshot from their church. She leads them to a trailer in a front lot belonging to Christopher Shepard.

"Hey, Shepard," Katrina says, a mischievous smile crossing her face.

He's nervously excited to see four 6th grade girls and a boy show up at his doorstep.

Katrina seems comfortable here, although Isabel, Joy, and Hope are not. Mickey seems indifferent—or maybe high.

"Hi, girls," Shepard says warily, but he lets them in.

Shepard's place looks like an old lady's house—filled with furniture he'd likely been given by his parents or collected from thrift.

"Hey, Shepard, you got any beer?" Katrina asks.

"Yes," he answers her coyly. "What about it?"

"Oh, you sly dog," Katrina says. "What about getting some for us? Nice place. Couch looks comfy."

"What makes you think I would serve beer to you five?" he asks playfully.

"Because we're thirsty, Shepard!" Katrina says. "We walked all this way out to see you, and now you should be a polite host and get us some beer."

Isabel, Joy, and Hope share panicked glances. They'd never intentionally held a conversation with Shepard—or really, any adult who wasn't a relative—and here Katrina was doing this cat and mouse thing, trying to secure some beer, which they didn't really want, anyway.

Mickey smiles, but honestly, Mickey is always smiling. And sweating.

"Do you all want some beer?" Shepard asks.

They all nod silently.

"Well, Mickey can have one because he's a boy, but no one else," Shepard decides.

"Actually, it's already late, Katrina," Isabel says. "We should get going."

"Oh, no," Katrina protests. "We just got here."

"Joy and Hope told their aunt they wouldn't be gone long," Isabel reminds her.

"See what you've done, Shepard?" Katrina teases. "If you'd been a better host, we'd all be able to stay and have a lovely time. But since you can't make us feel welcome, we're hitting the road."

The kids file out. Shepard watches the five leave, his expression a mix of relief and curiosity. He touches Joy's arm lightly.

"Come back when you can spend more time," he half whispers.

"Oh, man," Hope says back in the gravel lot with Shepard's place well behind her.

"What was that?" Isabel asks Katrina.

"He's a pretty good guy, I think, maybe," Katrina says. "We'll definitely be able to get him to buy us beer eventually."

"Have you been there before?" Hope asks her.

"Maybe..." Katrina grins.

Hope grimaces.

"I can't believe he was only going to give Mickey beer," Joy complains. "Because he's a boy. Can you believe that?!"

"Right," Mickey laughs. "He should have given everybody one."

"Except we're twelve!" Isabel laughs.

Mickey starts giggling, high-pitched and unruly. He can't stop. It infects the girls, and the whole lot stumbles toward Second Avenue, laughing almost uncontrollably.

"Still," Isabel says with an arm around Joy's neck. "The injustice of it!"

Joy laughs.

"I'm telling you, he will be the guy who buys us beer," Katrina promises. "Just give me a minute."

"I don't even like beer," Mickey says.

"Pot's OK, though," Isabel sneers.

Mickey ducks behind a tree.

"Oh my God, he's peeing," Isabel whispers.

Katrina rolls her eyes, but the rest of them erupt into shocked laughter.

They run ahead, dashing to the halfway point across Sandusky Bridge and putting some distance between them and the boy they have inexplicably hung out with all evening. The wind picks up, and the four huddle closer together as they walk.

As they hit the bottom of the bridge, they hear something from the other side of the trees.

"Caw caw, little birdies."

They can't see anyone, but the voice is male and slippery. The four girls look at each other and step into the street to move away from the bushes.

The bush shakes at them, and Katrina squeaks. Isabel looks at her, and all four chuckle until a figure emerges from the trees about four feet ahead of them.

He's skinny but grown, wearing only a tee-shirt despite the chill. The girls stop walking, and a second man pushes through the bushes behind them.

"Caw caw," he says with a hoarse laugh and slinks toward Katrina.

The raggedy man in front is walking toward the girls when Mickey calls from the top of the bridge.

"Hey, wait up!"

The bird caller turns his back to Katrina to yell, "Stay where you fucking are."

Joy tugs Hope and runs across Sandusky Street to the other side. The other kids follow.

Joy runs and runs until her side cramps. She slows down well into the neighborhood full of large, aging homes needing attention. They're almost to Apple Jack park, which means they have to walk past the Parkins house to get home.

Hope lopes up behind her sister. Joy's quicker, but Hope's long limbs make up ground.

Isabel is next. They can see Katrina and Mickey enter and exit the spotlight from the streetlamp a few yards away.

Joy bends forward and waits for her friends to pool around her.

"Oh man, what the fuck was that all about?" Katrina laughs.

No one else is laughing.

"Were they your brothers?" Isabel asks quite seriously.

Katrina shrugs it off.

"They live by the railroad tracks," Mickey says. "And that was totally them."

"Hannah says it might have been one of your brothers who jumped her coming home from Coney Castle the other day," Hope says.

Katrina shakes her head.

The friends resume walking.

"Who else would it be?" Isabel says.

They're almost to Apple Jack park.

"They can be dicks, I guess," Katrina finally says.

"We should tell your dad," Isabel suggests to Joy and Hope. "Maybe he'll call the police."

"Mom would never let him," Joy says.

"I don't think we need to involve the police," Katrina says as if re-enacting a crime show via dramatic reading.

Still, no one laughs.

Hope can see the rusty merry go round. The patchy grass and unkempt softball field lay so flat and neglected that the spare climbable equipment looks monstrous as the five pass.

Isabel looks around nervously.

"They'd ask what we were up to," Joy says calmly.

"They'd notice that Mickey was high," Hope says.

"I'm not high," Mickey responds quietly.

"Do you have pot in your pocket?" Isabel asks him.

"No."

"What would a drug-sniffing dog do if he smelled you?" Katrina asks.

Mickey tugs on his face.

"It probably wouldn't be that good," he says.

Hope can see the blackened driveway, the small wooden mailbox perched near the street, the hand-painted Dutch-inspired birds now faded with neglect: 116 Jackson Street.

"Right, plus what are we going to say we were doing?" Hope says. "Nothing to worry about, Mom. We were just at the choir teacher's double-wide trying to get him to give us some beer."

"No way that piece of shit trailer is double-wide," Katrina corrects, but they've stopped moving. All five are standing still and facing the Parkins place.

Kelly Parkins and her mom moved to Defiance back when Mr. Parkins went to prison. They never sold the house, just rented it out to different tenants over the years. The girls aren't sure if anyone lives there now, but the lawn is desperate for a mow.

"Sheriff says maybe Kelly Parkins should undergo memory regression therapy," Katrina states. "He says they still don't accept that the dad's the killer. They say it was Brenda's uncle. They still visit him and everything."

"What else are they going to do?" Hope asks. "He's her dad."

"Yeah, and a killer!" Katrina laughs. "Right back there."

She points around the house to a backyard too far and dark to truly see. Still, the other four shudder.

Hope shakes her head.

"Kelly says he was home with them watching Facts of Life."

"That's why she needs hypnosis!" Katrina laughs.

"Maybe if they hypnotized Mr. Parkins, they could get him to say what he did with Joannie Fabrizio," Isabel suggests.

Joy looks at Katrina.

"What are you even still doing here?" she asks. "We passed your street before we got to Apple Jack. You're going to have to walk all the way back to Sandusky Bridge by yourself."

Katrina smiles.

"Yeah, but I'm having a good time!"

Joy looks at Mickey.

"No way you think we're walking you all the way to 8th Avenue."

"Guess not," he shakes his head. "See ya!"

Mickey bolts up Jackson, past Stimmells' barn at the corner, and disappears.

Katrina sighs and turns to go back the way she came.

Joy, Hope, and Isabel start walking again.

"What is regression therapy?" Isabel asks.

"Bridget says it's like hypnosis, and it helps you remember stuff your brain has buried," Hope explains. "Hannah says it's bullshit."

"Bullshit," Joy confirms.

"It does feel kind of Scooby-Doo or something, right?" Isabel agrees. "Like, if a hypnotist can convince Charlie's Angels that they really want to be bank robbers, couldn't they also convince someone that their dad is a murderer?"

"Bridget says people remember being buried alive like with snakes and shit," Hope says. "She says Joy and I are really lucky we never had to go to a nursery school."

"Yeah, like staying with Hannah wasn't torture." Joy grins to herself, satisfied with her barb.

"Will you guys walk me home?" Isabel asks.

Hope and Joy frown.

"Please? There's two of you so you'll walk back home together. I'll be all by myself."

They wordlessly agree, turning together down the street between Stimmells' barn and Regina Oliver's green house. They take a right up Second Avenue that will run beyond the Murphy house, past the maple full of cawing birds, past the Gehrigs', past the Fabrizios', past the Cassidys', past Ray Ray's porch, where they wave at the indecipherable greeting from the old man in the rocker, to Isabel's front door.

"OK, bye!" she hollers as she bounds up the porch steps and in the door.

Joy and Hope dash back to 93 Second. They burst through the door, stop themselves and immediately try to hush their heartbeats and heavy breathing.

"What have you losers been up to?"

It's Hannah.

"We raced back from Isabel's house when we realized how late it was," Joy lies.

"That took much longer than expected," Mrs. Murphy says from her rocker. "Get ready for bed."

"You're lucky it's your birthday tomorrow," Hannah whispers. "Dad is pissed!"

The girls sneak upstairs and climb, fully dressed, into their bunk beds.

Hope falls asleep quickly and dreams of crows all lined up across the crucified arms of a scarecrow. One lands on its head then takes flight, the scarecrow's big straw hat in his claws. The scarecrow rolls its head and looks up at Hope. She realizes it's her mother hanging there, crows clutching her arms.

Easter Sunday

"Happy birthday, ugly girls!" Hannah says and hands Joy and Hope a gift-wrapped album.

Murphys are slowly making their way, couch to kitchen, bathroom to couch, all in different shades of readiness for the day.

"What can it be?" Joy mock-wonders.

"It's a toaster," Hannah confesses.

They open it. Business as Usual by Men at Work.

"Thanks, Hannah!" they say in unison.

"I kind of wanted the Go-Go's," Joy says.

"Yeah, they're cute," Hannah says. "Maybe for Christmas."

"Come on, now. We'll celebrate the twins after we celebrate Easter," Mrs. Murphy reprimands. She still looks a little weak to the girls. "Get ready for mass."

"You sure you'll be OK, Hope?" Hannah teases. "You're not feeling woozy, are you?"

She laughs. Everybody laughs.

Mrs. Murphy begins tutting her brood toward the door when the phone rings. She looks surprised at her husband, who shakes his head. She walks back to the kitchen to pick up the wall phone.

"Hello?"

She makes a surprised face.

"Happy Easter, Jo," she says, shooting her husband a look that says she knows we're headed to mass right now. Then her expression changes. She steadies herself on a kitchen chair.

"Oh my God," she says weakly.

Her eyes pass over the twins.

"Yes, she was," Mrs. Murphy says, looking toward Joy and Hope. "Yes, hard to hear on their birthday…"

"What?!" Hannah stage whispers.

Mrs. Murphy waves her off.

"Oh, no…" she says, suddenly full of concern. "It couldn't be him. He's—oh, poor Paulette…"

After a very brief pause, Mrs. Murphy shakes her head.

"You're so right, Jo," she corrects herself. "Poor Lois McCoy."

Hope and Joy suddenly pay attention.

Mrs. Murphy sighs.

"And they think he might have had something to do with Joannie all those years back?"

An anxious pause sees impatient girls staring at their mother.

"Thank you, Jo," Mrs. Murphy says finally. "I'm so sorry. I'm just so sorry this has to …ruin another Easter for you. Give Tony a hug for us."

Maureen Murphy hangs up the phone. She looks at her family, who stare with expectation toward her, and announces:

"We'll talk about it after mass."

"No!" comes a resounding response from her daughters.

"Be serious," Hannah commands.

Mrs. Murphy looks to her husband for support, but he stares as expectantly as his daughters.

"Well…" she looks at her daughters sadly. "Maybe this will give us all something to pray about."

Her eyes turn to Joy and Hope.

"Your little friend Katrina," she begins. She looks again at her husband as if to summon from him the wisdom on how to proceed. He walks to his wife, supports her arm, and looks at her curiously. "She's dead, girls. They found her in Stimmells' barn."

The air in the room disappears.

"What?!" Hannah reacts.

Mrs. Murphy sits, her husband taking her hand and shaking his head in horror.

"I guess there was a lot of blood pooling out from under the corner nearest the street," she says, her eyes on the floor. "Mrs. Cassidy noticed it during her morning walk, told Paulette about it, and the two investigated…they found her."

"This neighborhood is cursed," Hannah sighs.

Hannah's reaction isn't hard to understand. No one ever really got over the way little Brenda the Bug had been torn to pieces years ago, and the neighborhood still sometimes feels haunted, not by Joanie Fabrizio but by her absence. What happened to Katrina, though, was closer to what had happened to Brenda. She'd just been torn to shreds by a common garden trawler. Careful examination would suggest the work of more than one person. There was no sign that she'd been dragged into the place—doors weren't unduly disturbed, no signs of a ruckus at the entrances. It was as if she'd come in willingly or been lured. Not likely the kind of manipulation you'd expect from big, lumbering Eric Stimmell.

"They don't think it was Eric?" Mr. Murphy asks.

"They do."

"He wouldn't do that," he demands.

"He tried to kiss Hope!" Hannah responds. "He just walked in the house even though he didn't think anyone was home. How often do you think he does that—just comes on in?"

"He's not violent like that," Mr. Murphy says.

"He tried to kiss your 11-year-old daughter."

"Maybe it was Shepard," Hope says weakly.

"What?" Mr. Murphy asks.

"Why would you say that, Hope?" Mrs. Murphy asks her now sheepish youngest.

Hope looks at Joy, who almost imperceptibly shakes her head 'no.'

"Do not start throwing around accusations," James Murphy barks. "We don't do that."

"Next, they'll say Eric Stimmell's a witch," Maureen Murphy sighs.

"He's just a cripple," Hannah scoffs.

"Hannah!" Mrs. Murphy responds, shocked.

"That is why you're sure he didn't do it, isn't it?"

"Enough," Mr. Murphy announces.

"Maybe Eric Stimmell and Christopher Shepard are witches," Hannah says tartly.

Mr. Murphy turns to his daughter very seriously.

"Do not say things like that," he says gravely. "We don't say things like that."

"You notice, nothing like this ever happened in Odenton before Gaietto got there," Hannah points out.

Hope is feeling sick. Katrina is weird, and she talks them into doing things they really shouldn't do, but she's also lovely, and she smiles more than anyone Hope knows. She keeps thinking of what her mom said—blood pooling.

"Everyone, let's just go," Mrs. Murphy decides. "We'll be late for Easter mass."

Hannah takes Hope's hand, then Joy's. Hope cannot remember the last time Hannah held their hands, but she's doing it now, and they follow their dad through the living room.

As the cleaned and pressed Murphys solemnly single file it to their dad's station wagon, they notice a stranger on Regina Oliver's porch, next door. The house is dark. Regina doesn't have many guests. Even her big Italian family tends to stay away.

The man on the porch doesn't look like one of Regina's clan, anyway.

Hannah nudges Joy.

"Who's that guy?" she whispers.

Joy shrugs.

"Asshole Seth Oliver won't be happy," Hannah notes.

Mr. Murphy stops.

"Can we help you with something?" he inquires of the stranger.

The man smiles at Hope and Joy. He holds the smile for a beat, then faces Mr. Murphy.

"Good morning," he calls, walking to the edge of Regina's porch to better converse with the Murphys. "I'm working with your sheriff. I wanted to inquire whether your neighbor had seen or heard anything last night."

He pauses.

The stranger has an accent.

"Terrible about your other neighbor," he adds, throwing a glance toward the large barn looming behind him from across the street.

Mrs. Murphy looks away.

"Regina's probably at mass," James Murphy points out. "It's Easter Sunday."

"So it is," the stranger responds with some embarrassment. "I've lost track of myself. I appreciate your help."

He waves.

"Happy Easter," Mrs. Murphy says.

He turns and walks away from the Murphys.

It's hard to hear over the squawking of the birds in the maple, but it sounds to Hope like he says happy birthday.

Book 4: Fledgling
1988

Saturday, One Week to Easter Weekend

Hope lights a cigarette and slides the heavy silver lighter into her back pocket.

"Too bad we're not driving," Joy says flatly as she, her twin and their friend Isabel walk in the shadow of Odenton's big, decaying homes toward Coney Castle.

"What?" Isabel teases. "It's a lovely day for a stroll."

"Actually, we're still allowed to drive to work," Hope corrects her sister. "Technically. Legally."

"Right, but my mom probably wouldn't want me back in a car with you," Isabel says.

"What?!" Hope says. "It was your fault we were even at the party! I didn't know anybody."

"Yes," Isabel says with a wicked smile. "But you were the one in the driver's seat."

"It was parked," Joy says with tempered disdain.

"He's just always looking for me," Hope complains.

"You're just easy to find," Isabel decides. "It's because you're tall."

Hope frowns.

"Fucking Gaietto," Isabel responds with an exaggerated scowl.

"You almost had it!" Joy says to her.

"The Billy Idol face?" Hope asks.

"Super close."

Isabel brightens up.

Hope squints. Up ahead, moving toward them at a swagger, Howdy Noonan is not wearing a shirt. He's wearing jeans and cowboy boots but no shirt.

They cross the street to avoid bumping into him.

"Where is his shirt?" Isabel wants to know.

"He's probably heading to our neighborhood," Joy decides. "He won't need it."

"Surprised he's even wearing pants," Hope snorts.

They cross back over at Coney Castle, and Joy opens the heavy metal door at the rear of the store to a wave of odor: Coney sauce cooking in vats in the back of the building.

Isabel circles outside to the order window next to the giant metal ice cream cone around the front. There's only the cone now— the chocolate/vanilla twist ice cream top was blown off during a winter storm.

Isabel peeks between the taped-up paper signs advertising wares: coconut blizzards, chocolate chip wheelies, dipped cones, shredded chicken sandwiches. Joy looks back, opens the window. Hope hands a blue raspberry slurry through.

"Call me later," Isabel says cheerily. "Maybe I'll come to Regina's."

She walks back the way she came.

"Stir the meat every twenty minutes, turn the vat off at one. You can pull from it if you need to, but bucket the rest, cap it and get it into the walk-in."

Obie, the grim store owner, is re-explaining the process again to Cara Romig, who will graduate from the public high school this spring. She's staring contemptuously at the side of Obie's face and wearing an Iron Maiden tee shirt.

Hope sits on a stool near one order window and picks up a magazine with George Michael on the cover. Joy opens the drive-thru window for some air. It's too hot to be April. The small, tight building overheats quickly with the meat cooking in the back and this number of bodies inside. Plus, the smell of the meat gets to Joy.

Cara comes out front.

"Obie's off to Polar Pit."

Buster "Obie" Oberlin owns two ice cream stands. Coney Castle sits in a badly aging neighborhood on the north side of town. Polar Escape—or Polar Pit, as those left behind to work the lesser store disparage it— is a larger affair with fryers. It's located on the highway that leads out of Odenton. Obie spends most of his time there. There are more people driving out of Odenton than staying in.

"Nobody put out the hot fudge," Joy notices.

"Hope nobody wants it hot for a while," Cara says, returning to the back of the building. "I guess we could microwave it."

Hope jumps up, heads back with her.

"What would we pour it into?"

"Can't pour it – too thick. Just nuke it in the can," Cara suggests.

"No!" Joy laughs and shouts from the front of the building. "You'll blow the place up. Scoop it into a plastic tub."

She joins her co-workers in the back.

"Does that really happen?" Hope wonders aloud. "Does metal explode in a microwave?"

"Let's see," Cara decides with a grin. She pulls a large can from the shelf stocked with syrupy toppings, uses a standing can opener to remove the lid, and slides Fox's creamy rich Deluxe Milk Fudge into the microwave.

She looks at Hope tauntingly and closes the door.

"How long?" She poses the question to Hope, now her co-conspirator.

"Ten minutes?" Hope suggests.

Cara dials the microwave. It roars to life, the light inside allowing them to watch the can turn in circles, then spark, then spark some more.

The three girls scream.

Joy yells, "Turn it off!"

Hope reaches over, pops open the microwave door.

"Well, now we know," Hope declares.

"They say a dog will explode in there," Cara points out.

"Science!" Joy proclaims.

The back door opens. Dawn—well dressed, well-groomed, smiley—enters. No makeup, hair motionless and tipped in blonde, puffy socks gleaming white as they top her equally white high tops, everything on Dawn seems to sparkle. Her oversized, teal, bare-midriff tee reading PASTA is the only splash of color other than her amber tan.

Cara rolls her eyes.

"Hi, guys!" Dawn beams.

"I have drive-thru," Cara dictates. "Joy and Hope have the other two windows. You're late, so you do prep."

Dawn picks up a spoon and begins stirring the meat in vats on command. The others return to the front of the building. Cara opens the cash drawer at the drive-thru window, pulls out the twenties, and pockets them.

H&J pretend not to notice. Joy pulls an ice cream sandwich out of a trunk freezer, and Hope makes herself a chicken sandwich.

"You think we'll even have any business today," Hope says to no one in particular.

"Too early," Joy answers. "Nobody knows we're open for the season yet."

"No, we'll get a pop around noon, then die off," Cara predicts. "I'll probably leave after that."

The sisters look perplexed at each other. Cara makes a hot dog. Dawn walks out front.

Cara grimaces.

"Is your birthday tomorrow?" Dawn asks the sisters.

"No, next Sunday," Joy clarifies.

"Easter Sunday?" Cara mocks. "That must suck."

"It doesn't always fall on Easter," Hope says automatically.

"Mine's the perfect time—the end of May," Dawn specifies. "Everybody's still in school, so it doesn't get forgotten about, but it's nice and warm, so we can have our party outside before it's too hot. May is definitely the best month for a birthday."

Cara squeezes mustard on her hot dog and eyes Dawn. She sets her dog on the counter, picks up the ketchup, and says, in a falsely chipper voice, "Hey, Dawn!"

Dawn turns to her. The out-of-character brightness in the way Cara speaks draws the twins' attention.

Cara wields catsup in one hand, mustard in the other. She points toward PASTA and squeezes.

Dawn throws her hands up shield-like in front of her, but before she can step out of the way, Cara has her sopping with red and yellow from her elegant neck to her bare midriff and dripping down her tanned legs to her socks and shoes, white no longer.

Dawn stares, open-mouthed.

Hope starts pulling napkins from the dispenser, saying nothing.

Dawn blinks. She accepts Hope's napkins.

No one speaks for a long minute.

Dawn, wiping mustard from her chin and throat, says, with forced cheer, "OK, well...I guess I'll be back."

Cara looks at Hope. Hope and Joy begin to giggle, Cara laughs loudly. Through the drive-thru window, they watch Dawn walk through the side lawn dotted with picnic tables to a big house just past the edge of Coney Castle property, which she enters.

"That was fun," Cara says wistfully. She walks to the back and washes mustard from her hands.

A moment passes. Cara returns.

"I'm bored," Cara says. "I'll probably just bail. Cool?"

Hope nods.

By the time Dawn returns to Coney Castle, Cara and the business's inventory of twenty-dollar bills have long since exited for more interesting adventures. Business never does pick up.

Evening falls, the next shift arrives, and Hope and Joy walk through the rutted parking lot, past the rusting green dumpster toward the alley that leads home, the very one where Hannah was jumped six years ago. Hope carries two bags: one with chicken sandwiches, the other with chip wheelies.

"Choir practice again?" Hope asks her sister.

Joy nods.

"Are you taking the car?"

"No."

"You can," Hope says.

"Obviously," Joy responds drily. "It's not like you'll be using it."

They walk quietly down the alley and into their own small neighborhood.

Joy walks through the back door of 93 Second. Hope heads one door further to Regina Oliver's. She skirts between the two houses and onto Regina's large wooden front porch. She leans her head toward the screen of an open porch window.

"Bzz, bzz, bzz – Hey bumblebee!"

A cheerful "Come in!" returns from deep inside the house.

Regina vacuums the living room's shaggy brown carpeting, her two boys standing on the couch to play keep-away from the beast. Scott is almost 6. Nicholas is 10.

"Chicken sammies and chip wheelies!" Hope hollers.

"Yay!!" the boys cheer.

Regina brings the vacuum to a halt.

"You're the best."

"You're cleaning late," Hope notes, heading to the kitchen to put the ice cream treats in the freezer and debag the sandwiches. She grabs a Diet Coke from the fridge.

"Don't finish my pop," Regina warns. "Did you bring a movie?"

"Prince of Darkness," Hope says, returning from the kitchen and plopping into the thick, hot cushion of the couch. Little boys tumble about her.

"Is it scary?" Scott wants to know.

"I don't think so," Hope admits. "But maybe."

Regina smiles.

"Why do you only like scary stories?" Nicholas wonders.

"They're fun," Hope says. "Besides, they're useful. They make us feel better about real life because it's never as bad."

"But also, they make you see scary stories everywhere," Nicholas says.

Hope nods.

"And they give you bad dreams," Scott says.

Hope nods again.

"Do you like being scared all the time?" Nicholas asks.

"Not really," Hope admits.

It isn't long before boys are fed, cleaned, and offering Hope a goodnight hug.

"Are you coming over tomorrow?" Nicholas asks.

"Probably," Hope says, smiling.

"It's almost Hope and Joy's birthday," Regina beams. "They will be eighteen this Easter Sunday!"

"Just like you and Christmas," Nicholas says.

"Almost," Hope says. "Except Easter moves around, so my birthday is only on a holiday every so often. Your mom gets screwed yearly."

"Hope!" Regina laughs.

"Will you bring ice cream?" Scott wants to know.

"For my birthday?" Hope laughs.

"No, tomorrow," Scott clarifies.

"Sorry, buddy. I don't work tomorrow."

Regina ushers the boys upstairs and returns. She drops wearily into a chair, a puff of dust exploding as she does. But she smiles as always. Hope pops the tape in the VCR. Regina eyes Hope's beverage with suspicion then smiles.

"I needed this! Thanks, girl."

The film plays. Regina comes and goes, brings in a laundry basket, and starts folding. Hope watches with rapt attention while Donald Pleasance chews the scenery as a priest.

"I should watch this with Bridget," she says. "She only likes scary movies that are super Catholic."

"I'm not very sold on the Catholic angle here," Regina scoffs.

She's right. Pleasance is unconvincing.

"What is it about Catholic movies that's so creepy?" Regina wonders.

"We've been brainwashed to believe it could all happen. Sister Cleofa has us totally convinced."

Regina giggles.

"I don't even know Sister Cleofa," she says.

"Everybody has a Sister Cleofa,"

The phone rings. Hope pauses the movie.

Regina walks into the kitchen, picks up the green wall phone. She goes quiet. And then: "Hope's here, Seth. We just started a movie."

Regina walks to the entryway to the living room. It's Seth, she mouths to Hope and holds up one finger.

"Seth, can this wait?"

She looks perturbed, then sad. She walks back into the kitchen.

Hope sits quietly in the dark.

"I really don't know why you feel like you have to do this," Regina says.

After some time, Hope turns the movie back on. The guy from TV's Simon & Simon—Mustache, Hope has named him—plays the film's hero. He can't act.

Hope sometimes hears Regina cry during quiet parts in the movie.

Eventually, Hope turns off Prince of Darkness and sneaks out. The air on the porch has turned cool, and she wishes she'd brought a sweatshirt. She doesn't want to go into her house to grab one, cause a commotion. The lights are still on.

She gets into her Dodge Colt and drives to a drive-thru grocery store a block shy of Coney Castle.

"Diet Pepsi and Marlboro Lights."

She pulls out of the drive-thru and takes a right, heading back home, but doesn't turn onto Second Avenue. She continues on Sandusky Street, heading out toward the country.

She listens to Love and Rockets on tape and lights a cigarette. She rolls to a stop at the corner.

Headlights approach too quickly from behind her. She takes her foot off the brake, but before she can get out of the way, she's hit from behind. Her beloved Dodge Colt launches into the quiet intersection.

Hope's head snaps backward. She stares ahead at a flat, barren field. Her headlights pick out oversized crows landing in dirty rows.

An old song floats into her head.

Forevermore and evermore

Beneath the bush, behind the door

Fuzzy throat, little peep

Secret place, you and me

Chick, chick, chick, chick, chickadee

A man stands at her door. He is handsome. Older— maybe in his thirties, forties even. He's not dressed like Odenton.

She opens her door.

"Are you hurt?" he asks her.

He smells good, feels familiar, but there's no way she knows him. She swings one leg out of the car, then the other, then rests her head in her hands.

Another man sporting a flat top with a fringe of hair down his neck—a townie, obviously—gets out of his damaged car.

"I am so sorry!" he says. "This is totally my fault. I knew my brakes were going. This is totally my bad."

The first man asks again if Hope is all right and says they should phone somebody. The police? Her mother?

Hope holds up one hand, waving them off.

"Actually, I have to just go home," she says glumly.

"That's not a good idea," the handsome man tells her. He has an accent. "He's right, you know. I saw it all happen. It is his responsibility."

He touches her hand lightly.

"I'm driving without a license, so it doesn't matter," Hope says, standing now and paying little attention to the folks on the scene.

She looks at the rear of her car. It's bad. Really bad. The license plate is folded in half, the crease running right up the hatchback to the back window, so full of cracks it will likely drop in pieces right inside the vehicle if she blows on it.

She sighs.

"I have to go."

She limps the car to her house, parks out back, and creeps into her kitchen. The lights are out. She slips past her mom's hospital bed in the room at the bottom of the stairs, partly converted from her dad's office. His big desk is pushed into a corner, trophy parts and angels and dusty stopwatches casting weird shadows.

Hope sneaks up the dark steps, walks down the hall to her bedroom, and collapses, fully clothed, onto her bed, aging posters of Billy Idol, Duran Duran, and Prince staring down at her.

She looks out the window and watches the shadows cast by the streetlamp. She thinks of Eric Stimmell, lumbering down her stairs, enormous wings in his shadow. Birds line up on the still-naked maple branch, creating a giant birdy puppet show in the street. She watches the show until she falls asleep.

ROOST

Sunday

Hope wakes up a little nauseated. She's not sure if it's whiplash, shame, or worry over what will happen when her dad sees the car. She pushes herself up, kisses John Taylor of Duran Duran in the spot already worn from years of smooching, and stumbles downstairs to the shower.

A couple of hours drag like days, but mass is finally over at nearly lunchtime. Joy and Hope head to the station wagon while Mr. Murphy talks with Father Bowersox.

Joy takes co-pilot. Hope lays across the back seat, her feet and most of her shins sticking out the open back door.

"Why is it so hot?" Hope whines.

"Maybe next week Mom can come," Joy says. She unrolls her window.

"She won't like the new church," Hope says.

"Too modern," Joy agrees.

"I don't know why they didn't rebuild it to be the same," Hope says, propping herself up on her elbows. She gets a little dizzy and quickly returns her head to the cracking green vinyl of the back seat.

"Because it was a fire trap?" Joy offers.

"Not a Satanic fortress brought down by its own heathen anti-priest?" Hope mocks without opening her eyes.

"More like a candle-strewn tinderbox with an unsafe choir loft."

"Those steps probably went right up," Hope muses. "He'd have been totally trapped."

"What is our deal with candles, anyway?" Joy wonders.

"It's kind of a surprise it didn't happen sooner. Didn't you think those statues were marble, though?" Hope wonders. "I had no idea they were wood."

"They sure burned," Joy laughs. "Just like the martyrs of old."

"It's so weird how everybody chalks it up to Satan if they don't like the person. Every time something terrible happens, they pick on one person who's a little weird instead of—"

"Christopher Shepard was very weird," Joy interrupts her.

"Right, but surely he wasn't Black Mass weird," Hope says. "He probably kicked over a candle or something. I don't think the devil would even want him."

"Well, he has him now."

Hope laughs.

"Still, the church seems creepy now."

"Shepard probably haunts it," Joy guesses. "All Phantom of the Opera style."

Mr. Murphy finally joins them, so Hope sits up and closes her door.

"Church looks good," he decides. Hope and Joy don't argue. Joy points as a cardinal dips from the church eaves and leads the Murphy car out of the parking lot.

Pulling up to 93 Second, the three see Hannah's car out front.

"I hope Bernard's with her," Mr. Murphy says grumpily. "That desk is heavy."

"We're plenty strong," Hope says.

Her dad ignores her.

Hannah's home to help finish cleaning out Mr. Murphy's office and turn it into a proper spot for their mom. Mrs. Murphy can't make it up and down the stairs anymore; besides, it's already getting too hot upstairs, making it harder for her to breathe. She'll be cooler downstairs, and when summer comes, if it's necessary, they can invest in some window unit air conditioners.

Mrs. Murphy's dozing in the big blue chair, an empty violet vase forgotten and dusty on the end table next to her. Her nurse reads a People magazine in the rocker near her.

The trio quiets down as they enter. Joy looks past the nurse toward the kitchen. Hannah has the 409 spray out and is tackling the stovetop.

"Hey, losers," she whispers cheerily.

Mrs. Murphy grabs Joy's sleeve gently as she walks past.

"Mom's awake," Joy calls, and Hannah moves into the living room.

"Hi, Mom," she says.

Mrs. Murphy smiles.

"Did you forget Hannah was coming?" Hope asks.

Hannah bends down to kiss her mom as someone knocks at the door.

Joy answers it. Over her shoulder, Hope can see Honey Gehrig on the porch with a casserole.

"Hi, Honey," Hannah says brightly from the living room.

The Murphys' neighbor walks timidly, casserole forward, into the living room.

"I thought I saw you walk up, Hannah," Honey Gehrig says. "I don't want to bother you, but I thought I'd bring over some chicken and noodles."

"That's so nice!" Hannah says, taking the dish. Honey turns to Mrs. Murphy.

"How are you feeling, Maureen?" she asks.

Mrs. Murphy reaches for Honey's hand.

"How are the girls?" Hannah asks her.

"Not too bad," Honey replies. "Hank has them in a private school outside Cincinnati. It's Kentucky, technically, but it's a nice area."

Mrs. Murphy smiles.

"Have a seat," Hannah tells her. "We're going to clean out Dad's office, but if you want to keep Mom company for a while, that would be great."

"Can I help?" she asks.

"Oh, it's a nasty job," Hannah tells her.

"I'm pretty sturdy," she says, following the group—minus Mr. Murphy, who poured himself a cup of coffee and is now relaxing on the couch.

Hannah opens the dusty curtains, and the four survey the cluttered wreck of an office, a hospital bed crowded depressingly in the corner.

Hannah says quietly to her sisters, "You guys need to look after Dad."

"I feel like maybe he could look after us," Joy responds flatly.

"Did you get kittens?" Hope asks Honey.

"Well, I found them," Honey smiles. "I heard these tiny mews, and when I opened the storage closet, there they were, in a mashed up old grocery sack. Four of them."

"Cute!" Hannah says.

"There's a space, a nook, under the door. I guess that's how the mama cat was getting in and out. But she doesn't come by anymore, so I'm the mama now."

In the light, Hope realizes that what she had chalked up to dark circles may, in fact, be bruises on Honey Gehrig's face.

"Howdy does not like them."

"Howdy?" Hannah asks.

"Her tenant," Joy says.

"He complains about the noise—says it echoes up the steps and sounds spooky up in his room," Honey Gehrig says. "I told him to just grow up."

Hope nods, looks away from Honey's bruised face, and the four begin un-piling Mr. Murphy's junk from the top of his desk.

Tuesday

The sun begins to set as Hope and Isabel and half a dozen high school boys and girls load into the back of Strawberry Carl's old pick up with bags and bags of toilet paper.

"Where's Joy?" Isabel asks.

"Choir practice," Hope tells her.

"Again?"

Hope shrugs.

"What's choir got that we don't?" Isabel wonders.

"Not toilet paper," Hope responds, pulling a four-pack out to use as a pillow behind her back.

"Correct," Isabel agrees. "We have all the toilet paper."

"All of it."

"Where first?" Strawberry Carl calls from the driver's window.

"JP Young's house," Isabel commands. Hope looks at her, and Isabel smiles wickedly. "He fucking deserves it."

"I didn't think you even cared. You totally aimed too low with him."

"Yeah, but fuck him, though," Isabel says.

"True enough."

It's not yet dark. Friends begin tearing rolls from plastic wrapping, Strawberry slows down at a corner, Isabel confirms that this is the place. Calvary High School kids spill out of the back of the pick-up to begin tossing rolls into trees, over bushes, atop the garage, and over eaves.

Hope and Isabel laugh.

A light comes on in JP Young's house.

The two girls freeze.

The back door opens.

Calvary High School kids run toward the pick-up and throw themselves in.

Hope looks up. Isabel is gone. Hope looks around, scans the periphery before running. She sees Isabel—safely perched in Strawberry's truck bed.

Hope takes her first leaping step toward the truck when someone grabs her by the waist of her jeans, halting her forward progress. She struggles against the grip and watches the vehicle pull away.

Hope is in the yard alone with JP Young's dad.

As the pick-up takes off and other teens scatter through the neighborhood, Hope's pulled backward by her belt loop. She drops suddenly into a squat, breaking Young's grip, but he wraps an arm around her middle, turns her toward his house, grips her neck with his other hand, and marches her through his screened back door and into his kitchen.

He stops in the light of the kitchen and gives her a look.

"I know you," he shouts, full of exasperation. "You go to Calvary."

He pushes her against his refrigerator and lets go.

"Tee-peeing is vandalism," he tells her, grabbing paper and pen from a table by a wall phone. "Now, you will write down the names and phone numbers of everyone else who was in that truck."

Hope stares blankly ahead—not at him, not at anything.

He yells in her face.

"You will tell me who else was with you!"

She stares. Her eyes are at half-mast. She is calm. Unperturbed.

"Oh, is that how you want to play it?" he asks.

Mr. Young picks up his wall phone and dials, nodding toward Hope and mumbling, "Uh-huh."

"Joe?" he perks up. "Doug Young. Some hoodlums from your school just trashed my front yard. I have one of them with me here, and I think she has something to say to you."

He hands her the phone, smirking.

"Joe Mooney – your principal."

She takes the phone, says nothing. She doesn't hold it to her face; she only stares.

Doug Young grabs the phone back.

"Jesus Christ," he says into the receiver. "It's one of the Murphy girls. Ask her who was in the goddamn truck."

He holds the phone up to her ear.

"Is this Hope?"

She sighs.

"Hope, you're in some trouble here," principal Joe Mooney says calmly. "Let's just get this over with quickly, all right? Let's not cause your mom and dad any extra worry. Just tell me, who was in the truck?"

"I don't know, Joe," Hope says, monotone. "Public school kids."

Irate and flabbergasted, Doug Young takes the phone back, banging it into its wall cradle without speaking again to Principal Mooney.

Hope stares past him toward a dark window above the breakfast nook in the back of the kitchen. She sees the outline of a large bird landing on the ledge.

Doug Young paces in his kitchen, eyeing first Hope and then the floor.

Her eyes wander the kitchen to the microwave, the blender, the knife rack, an open cellar door. Time passes in this way, Doug Young and the silent high school girl alone with him in his kitchen. His expression turns from anger to discomfort.

"Just go," he tells her. "If this ever happens to my house again, I will send the police to your house. We'll see how your mom and dad feel about this."

Hope sighs. For the first time, she makes eye contact with Doug Young. Her look is disdainful, then dismissive. She lingers in his kitchen, eyes fixed and judging.

Doug Young moves his weight from one foot to the other, looks at her, then looks uncomfortably around the room.

She draws a breath, pauses. She takes a deliberate step toward him. Then leaves through the screen door.

Hope begins walking. A light rain mists the spring air, and the sidewalks are dark because of all the trees. She decides to walk in the street. Light from the streetlamps bounces off the water moistening the asphalt. The streets of Odenton are quiet. Hope's shadow in this light seems too big to her—winged, even. She's reminded of something she can't quite reach.

She likes the idea of a massive pair of wings, though. It's soothing. She could fly home. She could just fly off.

Her walk takes some time. Back at home, Hope's dad is upset.

Joy is home, giving Hope the stink eye.

"What the hell happened to the car?!" he yells.

Hope says nothing.

"She didn't have it," Joy reminds him. "She was out with Isabel."

"Well, your car is beat to hell! God damn it!"

He paces in the kitchen, then: "Someone must have rammed it tearing down the back alley and just took off and left it!"

Hope's mood brightens slightly—case solved!

James Murphy mumbles "horseshit" under his breath and turns toward the living room. Alone, Joy gives her sister a suspicious glance.

"What?"

Joy rolls her eyes.

Wednesday

Hope and the boys sit on Regina's couch, sweating in an unseasonable hot spell and watching Charles in Charge on the big console TV.

"Scott! Get off me," Nicholas complains.

"Seriously, buddy, it's too hot to lay on people," Hope tells him.

Scott makes a whining noise.

"Scott, stop!" Nicholas whines.

"Whyyyyyy is it soooo hotttttt?" Hope whines back at them. She collapses as if boneless and slides to the floor. The boys giggle.

The phone rings. It's Regina.

"Can you do me a big favor?" Regina asks. "Make some ice—and pick up whatever toys you and the boys have scattered around on the floor?"

"Oh, that's right—today's your party," Hope glances toward the Transformers and Thunder Cats littering the living room and dining room floors, couches, tables. "On it, lady."

"All right, youngsters," Hope announces, turning off the TV. "We have a mission."

Nicholas drags out the sticker-covered plastic buckets. Scott, easily distracted, helps by not getting more toys out of the endlessly tempting buckets. Hope fills ice cube trays.

Tasks accomplished, Hope drops in a heap on the shag, and all three turn their bleary attention back to the TV.

Regina walks through the door, rousing them from their sweaty stupor.

"Hey, guys!" Regina says merrily.

"Mom!" the boys wearily cheer.

Regina walks in front of them and switches off the TV.

"Why do you watch this junk?" she asks.

"Scott Baio is a misunderstood genius," Hope responds.

"Boys, go wash up. I'm going to start some dinner," she says, asking Hope, "You staying?"

"Yep."

A short time later, the four sit around a hand-me-down round table with a cheery plastic gingham tablecloth, each with a plate of lasagna.

"I think people are taking the sheriff and his pet project seriously," Regina says conspiratorially to Hope.

"The whole—"

Regina clears her throat dramatically, eyeballing her impressionable boys.

"The whole dirt devil carpet cleaning thing?" Hope asks.

Regina chuckles.

"Yes. The dirt devil carpet cleaning business. He brought in a specialist, an outside investigator. A Ph.D. He's going to be part of our visiting scholar series at OU."

"No way!" Hope says. "Odenton University brought in a Dr. Van Helsing? What a bunch of maroons."

"I don't know. He seems very savvy."

"You met him?" Hope's interest is piqued.

"I did. They had a little lunch reception for him. You, of all people, would like him. Trust me."

"And he doesn't think Gaietto is a rube?" Hope is skeptical. "Because that's probably a non-negotiable for me."

Regina chuckles.

"He'll be here later. He's fascinating. Very worldly."

"You have a crush!"

Nicholas and Scott look up. Hope recovers.

"On Scott Baio! That's it! That's why you won't let us watch Charles in Charge. You're jealous!"

Nicholas disagrees.

"That's dumb."

"You don't think she loves Scott Baio?" Hope asks him. "Because I think you love his girlfriend, Gwen."

Scott laughs. Nicholas turns red.

"I do not!"

Regina chuckles.

"That crazy Hope. She never knows what she's talking about, does she?"

Eventually, Regina gets the boys ready for bed. Puts them to bed. Comes downstairs.

Hope is still sitting on her couch.

Guests began arriving. Hope looks on smiling. She is not dressed for a party, has not even showered. She is too young for this party, and yet there she is, eating chips and taking up space on the couch.

Regina barely notices. She's so used to having Hope in her house. It's like forgetting that your refrigerator makes a constant humming noise or that your toilet handle has to be jiggled.

Hope moves to the front porch as the party progresses when a middle-aged blonde comes out for a smoke.

"Hello," Blonde says.

"Hi."

"You're Regina's babysitter?"

"Yep."

"And—why are you here? Now, I mean?"

"I'm pretty much always here."

Hope could see her own house just a handful of feet away from Regina's porch if she'd look. Could see her own bedroom window, her parent's darkened bedroom window over the front porch roof, the brand-new air-conditioning unit in the window to what was once their dad's office. But she doesn't look.

"Well, I was just thinking about a dream I had," the blonde says, giving Hope a little mischievous glance. "I think dreams are fascinating, don't you? The rules, the logic—you can be so frightened in a dream, but why? What is there to be afraid of? Nothing can hurt you. You can't die in a dream."

"Oh, you can," Hope says matter-of-factly. "I have."

"No, you haven't."

"I have," Hope says. "I have these dreams sometimes that I'm a vampire. I can't fly, really, though. I kind of hover, but to move fast, I have to kind of claw at the earth and push myself forward. And I go to the grocery store a lot—that's where I kill people. Usually, that guy who played Skipper on Gilligan's Island. Or one time Cher. Or Richard Dawson from Family Feud. But one time, I was in my front yard. A wolfman dragged me under that porch," she points to Gehrigs' porch. "Killed me."

Blonde grimaces.

"So, you don't really die if you dream it. Obviously. People always say that, but they don't know what they're talking about."

A man has come onto the porch. Hope didn't see the door open, didn't see him climb the porch stairs, but he's standing quietly behind the two.

Blonde walks inside, calling for Regina.

"I don't think she liked your story," the man says from the shadow. He has an accent. His tone is conspiratorial.

Hope squeezes past him and moves inside.

"I cannot believe you leave your children alone with her," Blonde is admonishing Regina. "Is she that Murphy girl? With everything happening in this town, you'd be wise to rethink the kind of dark influences you let into this house."

Regina scoffs. Blonde notices Hope.

"I just think that it's such a lovely evening. Maybe it's time your morbid teenage neighbor goes home," Blonde says to Regina.

Regina reaches past Blonde to give Hope a squeeze.

"Oh, I wouldn't recognize the place without Hope here."

Blonde stalks off, and Regina asks, all smiling curiosity, "What did you say to her?"

"I think we were talking about those vampire dreams I have?" Hope offers.

"Well, that is perfect party banter," Regina says. She shakes her head and chuckles.

"Who's that dude?" Hope motions toward the front porch.

Regina walks to the door, then opens it. Hope hasn't moved. Regina looks back and gestures for her to follow.

"Hiya, Victor," Regina says to the intriguing man on the porch.

Hope follows, quietly shrinking. The man smiles warmly at Hope.

"This is Hope," Regina introduces.

"We've met," Victor says. "Just now. She is exactly as you described her. She was frightening one of your guests with tales of blood and death."

He winks.

"Sounds about right," Regina laughs.

"I should probably hit it," Hope says to Regina.

"You're going?"

"So soon," Victor says, disappointed.

"Yeah," she says, still speaking only to Regina. "Go check on my mom."

"How is your mother?" Victor asks Hope. Startled, she looks directly at him for the first time. "Regina mentioned she's not well."

Hope doesn't respond.

"And your sister? Regina tells me there's a second one of you."

He smiles warmly. Hope feels a little sick.

"So, I'll see ya, then," she says to Regina.

"Hope!" Regina calls, surprised, but Hope makes a break for it, dashing down the porch steps and across the two front lawns. The Gehrigs' porch catches her eye, and she looks into the darkness of the latticework beneath, then mounts the concrete front steps of 93 Second and walks inside.

Hope stands silently in the dark and listens to the rasp and click of her mom's new ventilator in the next room. Otherwise, the house is quiet. She moves silently toward her dad's office to head up to her room but notices him there. James Murphy has climbed fully clothed into the hospital bed to spoon with his wife and fallen asleep, his eyeglasses pushed into an angle that seems terribly uncomfortable.

They look like twins in a womb.

She's afraid she might wake one of them if she sneaks past, so she walks outside to sleep in her car. She stares through the front windshield—the back windshield now fitted with cardboard—and tries to picture the wolfman but can only see the outline of a giant bird.

Thursday

Hope unlocks Regina's front door, two very sticky little boys trailing behind her.

"Man, I knew those bomb pops were a bad idea."

"A delicious mistake," Nicholas pronounces, and Hope laughs out loud.

"Just go stand in the tub, both of you, and don't touch anything. We'll have a quick wipe down before anything nice sticks to you."

They're heading back into the living room and debating their viewing options—VHS rental of Monster Squad or the tail end of Jem on TV—when the doorbell rings.

Hope freezes. The three of them look at each other.

"Since when do you guys have visitors?"

The boys shrug.

"Maybe it's one of your friends," Scott suggests.

"Hope's friends just walk in."

The bell rings again.

Scott shrugs.

"Why don't you just answer it?"

She smiles at the boys, and the three dash to the front door together. Nicholas moves the curtain.

It's Victor.

"He's so early," Hope whispers.

"We should let him in," Nicholas whispers back.

Hope sighs and opens the door.

"Regina isn't home from work yet."

Long pause.

"But you can come in…"

"Thanks terribly," he says warmly, moving into the front room.

Victor looks directly at Hope, into her face. She blushes. He extends his hand for a shake, and Hope accepts. His grip is cool and smooth.

Victor is gorgeous. Hope tries not to look at him. Worse still, he smells good. Hope tries not to smell him.

"Look what we have!" Scott shouts, pulling Victor's hand, then releasing and running for a Transformer. He dumps the bucket in the search.

"Guess I'll go home, then," Hope says.
Victor laughs.

"I appreciate your confidence, but I'm not sure I'm qualified for the job."

He throws a glance toward the boys. Scott is still digging. Nicholas is sorting through the Transformers on the floor to help.

"It's actually a great trust she puts in you. I find something very fierce and comforting in seeing caregivers looking after someone so vulnerable and small."

"They're pretty tough," Hope responds nonchalantly.

"I can't find him, but this guy's cool, too," Scott shouts, and Victor glides into the living room to stoop down and see.

Hope drags in after, not sure what to do precisely. She sits on the couch. Victor pats Scott's head then sits as well.

"What do you plan to do after high school? Stay in Odenton?"

Awesome. Banter.

"Good lord, no."

Victor smiles.

"And what about your sister? Will she stay?"

"Joy? Oh, hell no."

"Won't one of you need to stay behind and look after your parents?"

Hope doesn't respond. She looks at the coffee table, notices her breath has gotten shallow.

"How will you pay for college?"

"We're not cut out to be the people who stay in Odenton."

"Like Regina?"

She really feels short of breath.

"Or your parents. Surely, it's not so bad. They seem fulfilled here, don't they?"

"It's just not my bag."

"I wonder. It's more of a sacrifice—leaving—than you realize. I wonder what you're honestly prepared to give up to leave Odenton behind."

She still isn't looking at him, and now she's just stopped responding to him. She considers getting on the floor with the boys when she hears the kitchen door.

Regina's here.

"Oh, you're here!" Regina says to Victor, who rises as the boys rush in for their hug. "Let me just put my stuff down, and we can run."

She squeezes her boys. "Are you two going to have fun with Hope tonight?"

"Yeah!" they yell.

"We have a scary movie," Scott whispers.

"You do?!" Regina responds, looking with a little warning toward Hope.

"Harmless," Hope tells her. "Totally harmless."

"It was so nice to see you again, Hope," Victor tells her. He looks at her a long while and says, "I feel as if I know you, as if we met before last night."

Hope thinks of her car accident.

Regina chuckles.

"The Murphys don't do a lot of world traveling," she says. "Unless you've been to Odenton before."

"Oh, I have, actually," he says.

"Have you?!" Regina is surprised to hear it.

"A couple of times," he clarifies. "Every few years, the sheriff beats the drum, and I come dancing."

He looks at Hope.

Hope stares dumbly at the brown shag, noticing the Cheez-It bits she and the boys left peppered around the floor yesterday. She thinks that it wouldn't kill her to run the vacuum once in a while before Regina gets home, but Victor interrupts her thoughts.

"I find myself sort of drawn here," he says and turns his eyes to Regina, smiling.

"Oh, you old smoothie!" Regina laughs.

Victor laughs as well.

Hope wonders aloud: "You study Satanic cults?"

Regina looks surprised. Victor does not.

"Not exactly," he says. "Your sheriff does. I think his work is…provocative."

"So easy to avoid logic when you can blame a boogeyman instead," Hope blurts. It's her mother coming out of her, but she's immediately sorry she's made Regina uncomfortable.

Victor smiles.

"How is your mother?" Victor asks.

Startled, Hope stares silently.

"Well, we should probably get a move on," Regina says brightly to the group. "Hugs!" she says to the boys, who comply.

Regina and Victor pass through the kitchen and out the door to the garage, and Hope says to Nicholas and Scott, "Who's hungry?"

She rummages around the pantry.

"Let's get pizza," Scott suggests.

But Hope has discovered a personal favorite.

"Ooooo – canned ravioli!"

"Pizza!" Scott demands.

"No, sorry," she says, clearly not sorry. "We're totally having this."

"I think Mom wanted you to warm up the Sloppy Joe in the refrigerator," Nicholas reports.

"Yuck. No. Ravioli." Hope decides.

She pours the contents of the large can into a pot and sets it on a burner but absent-mindedly turns on a different burner—one that sits under a frying pan with the grease from lunch in it.

"Uncle Bob says we should watch GI Joe instead of Jem," Scott tattles.

"No way," Hope decides. "Totally fascist. Although, what is the deal with Jem, anyway?"

"She's truly outrageous," Nicholas clarifies.

Behind her, the frying pan heats.

"She is that," Hope agrees. "I like where your head's at, Oliver. But I mean the villains."

"The Misfits," Scott lisps.

"Right? Jem's nemesis is a punk band called The Misfits," Hope says with disbelief.

"So?" Scott wants to know.

"So, there already is a punk band called The Misfits, and they're not a bunch of illiterate girls with green hair. Glenn Danzig should sue. Also, why is the world so against misfits? What's a misfit ever done to the world?"

"I like He-Man better," Scott says.

"He-Man does have a better villain," Nicholas agrees.

With an almost soundless pop, the grease in the frying pan behind them ignites.

"Skeletor is the best!" Scott cheers.

"Mumra's the best cartoon villain," Hope counters.

"No way! Skeletor!" Scott shouts.

"Nicholas, tie break?" Hope asks.

Nicholas looks up—points to the stove.

Flames.

"Oh, shit." Hope darts toward the blaze, turns off the burner. "Fuck. Hey, no problems here. Why don't you guys go to my house for a minute?"

The boys run out the front door.

"What do you put a fire out with?" Hope asks herself out loud. She puts her head back in the pantry. "Baking something—baking powder? Soda? Flour?"

Hope's dad barges in the front door, cursing under his breath. He heads directly for the sink.

"It's a grease fire, Dad," she states over her shoulder.

Still mumbling, Mr. Murphy fills a pan with water.

"Dad!" Hope is suddenly panicked. "It's a GREASE FIRE!"

Nothing.

"It's a grease fire, Dad! Grease fire! Grease fire!"

Mr. Murphy pours the water onto the grease fire.

The flame in the pan blues and rolls ceiling-ward, melting the plastic window curtains above the sink as it moves. Then, spectacularly, it burns itself out.

Hope stands frozen.

Her dad shakes his head. He rubs his face with his hands, looks at his daughter briefly, shakes his head again, and leaves.

Hope stares, silently bewildered, as he goes.

"Crisis averted, then," she says to no one. "Thanks for the assist."

She looks at the charred mess, gets a bit sick to her stomach. Hannah would know what to do, she thinks as she surveys the damage. At least Hannah would know the best way to clean up the wreckage before Regina gets home.

After a minute, Hope walks to the phone. She picks it up, realizes she doesn't have a number to call, and hangs up. Unable to call Regina—or her mom, Hannah or even Joy, for that matter—she calls Isabel.

No one answers.

Sometime later, the burnt kitchen curtains are down, there are scrub marks in the black from the fire on the kitchen walls. Hope and the boys sit around the kitchen table, a half-empty pizza box in front of them.

"We could tell Gramma," Scott suggests.

"That would only panic someone else, and your mom still wouldn't know. I'll just wait until she gets home and tell her then."

"She won't be mad at you," Nicholas says, trying to comfort Hope.

"Oh, yes, she will," Scott corrects him.

"Scott! It wasn't Hope's fault," Nicholas reasons. "Mr. Murphy did it."

"Hope started it," Scott says. "Mr. Murphy just made it worse."

Hope sighs.

"And that's why you don't trust your family to Murphys. Go brush your teeth, dudes. It's almost time."

There's a knock at the front porch screen door. It's Sheriff Gaietto.

Hope hesitates, but Scott runs for the door.

"Hey, little man," Gaietto smiles. "Heard you had a little fire over here."

Scott strains to get the door open on his own, rambling excitedly.

"Yeah! Hope started a fire, and Mr. Murphy came over and made it worse!"

Gaietto moves past the boy, looks up the staircase, into the living room, and walks toward the kitchen.

"Is that right?" he asks.

He comes to a stop at the kitchen table, smiles insincerely at Hope, and takes in the unconvincing cleaning job above and around the stove. He waves his hands in front of his nose.

"Kinda stinks in here," he says.

Hope doesn't move. She looks at the boys – Scott still trailing the sheriff, Nicholas frozen halfway between the dinner table and the bathroom, pajamas in hand. Hope reaches her hand out toward him.

"Looks pretty tasty," Sheriff says, nodding at what's left of the pizza. "Mind?" He helps himself, and Nicholas slips behind Hope's chair.

"I wanted pizza, but Hope wanted ravioli," Scott says. "It burnt up, so we had pizza."

"That so?" he asks. He sits at the table and looks to Hope. "Maybe you could fill in a few details?"

"Who called you?" Hope wants to know.

"That matter?" He tosses his slice back into the box. "Why don't you tell me what really happened?"

"You should tell him," Scott says from across the kitchen. "He's the police."

"Scott!" Nicholas shushes him. "You don't have to tell the police everything."

Sheriff Gaietto snorts.

"Is that what your babysitter teaches you?"

"Don't talk to the boys," Hope tells him. "Boys, go get ready. Brush your teeth, go to the bathroom, get your pajamas on, then call me."

"Oh, I think they should stay put," Gaietto says.

"Well, you're not in charge here." She pats Nicholas's behind. "Go."

Nicholas collects his brother, and the two disappear into the bathroom.

"Fire, huh?" Gaietto nods. "Wonder what made you decide to play with fire."

"Well, grease doesn't catch snow, right?" She's staring past him to the big window in the next room that lines up with her own house. "Who called you?"

"What does it matter?" he says. "Neighbors are concerned. Do they have a reason to be?"

"I don't feel like you should be here," she says somewhat weakly. Everything out the window is still.

He leans in. "Is that right?"

She slaps the table decisively.

"Yes," she says. "I'll just get the boys, and we can talk next door."

He leans back.

"You sure you want to bother your poor parents with this?"

"Definitely," she says. "Boys? You close?"

"Still pooping," Scott shouts from the bathroom.

The sheriff stands.

"Guess I'll be the one who considers your parents' feelings, then," Gaietto says. He pushes his chair in, taps the table, and slowly makes his way toward the front door.

He turns back as he opens.

"I guess I'll be—"

"Yeah, yeah, yeah," she waves him off and turns toward the bathroom.

"You know who else plays with fire?"

She freezes.

"Satan," he chuckles. "Satan likes it real hot."

"Are you fucking kidding me?" she says, turning toward him. "What is wrong with you?"

Sheriff Gaietto looks startled by her response. He pauses for a second, and when she takes a step toward him, he leaves.

After she gets the boys read to and tucked in, Hope descends the carpeted steps, pops a VHS tape of Angel Heart into the VCR, and settles into Regina's plushy couch in the dark. It stars Mickey Rourke and Robert DeNiro, notorious because of a sex scene, but she's hoping it's scary.

The phone rings.

Hope pauses the movie, picks up the phone. Before she can say hello, she hears a high, whiny male voice.

"Regina?"

It's Seth, Regina's ex.

"No. This is Hope. Regina's not here."

"Where the hell is she?"

"I'm not at liberty to say," Hope smiles.

"What the fuck does that mean?"

"I have to go now."

Hope hangs up, looks a little freaked, goes back to her movie.

The phone rings again.

"No fucking way," she mutters.

She answers the phone.

"Where the fuck is my wife?"

Hope hangs up.

The phone rings again.

The calls are coming from inside the house, Hope thinks. She unplugs the phone.

Within 15 minutes, Hope hears the loud engine of a midlife crisis muscle car outside. Wuss-metal plays too loudly. Hope peeks out the window.

It's Seth.

He sits, his car running, parked in front of Stimmells' barn, bad music pouring out of his T-top.

Hope drums her fingers nervously on the back of the couch. She gets back up, looks again, paces a bit. She plugs in the phone. Then, for the second time tonight, she calls Isabel.

This time she's home.

"Dude, Seth Oliver is sitting outside in his car."

"Is he coming in?" Isabel asks.

"I don't know. He's just sitting there, playing crappy music and sitting there."

"Like a stalker?"

"Yeah, totally freaking me out," Hope admits.

"What's Pervy listening to, 'Let's Go All the Way'?" Isabel laughs.

"No, it's that bad White Snake song," Hope whines. "The muscle car one."

"Hey! I like that song."

"I think it's Motley Crue now," Hope strains to hear.

"What about that Alice Cooper Friday the 13th song?" Isabel says. "That would be creepier."

"Motley Crue sucks so hard," Hope bitches. "They will be remembered as the worst band in the world."

The music stops.

"Eep!" Hope squeaks. "The music stopped. I think he's coming in!"

"Don't let him in. I'm coming over."

"Dude, you are the best!"

Hope hits the lights, double checks the lock on the door, and returns to the couch to sit nervously. His motor is quiet now, but the words to Alice Cooper's "Man Behind the Mask" creep into Hope's head.

"Thanks, Isabel. What a fucking terrible song," she says to no one. "And still, weirdly creepy."

She hears a rustle on the front porch.

"Bzz bzz, Bumble, let me in," Isabel says through the open window.

Hope opens the door, but Isabel doesn't come all the way in. She stands in the doorway and looks toward Seth's car, assessing the situation.

"Dude, did you run?"

"It's dark and scary out here!" Isabel says. "Has he been there the whole time?"

"Yes, and his musical taste remains suspect."

Isabel listens. Loverboy, "Lovin' Every Minute of It."

"Holy lord," Hope groans. "Did he make himself a mixtape of every bad song ever recorded?"

"Maybe his girlfriend made it for him," Isabel says slyly, stepping boldly to the edge of the porch to better stare at the car.

"He is not dating Cara Romig," Hope decides. "No way. Cara would slaughter a Loverboy fan in their sleep."

"He's dating a teenage drug dealer," Isabel says. "How many teenage girl drug dealers do you think there are in Odenton?" Then she shouts toward the street, "Hey!"

Hope panics a little.

Isabel laughs. She's yelling now.

"Hey, creepy! Take off, man, or we'll call the police."

Hope tries to look calm, formidable even.

"What's he doing?" Hope asks.

"Is he opening his door?" Isabel wonders.

"Let's go inside." Hope pulls Isabel by the arm. She shakes Hope off and walks off the porch toward Seth's car.

"Fuck, fuck, fuck, fuck, fuck," Hope chants without realizing. She walks inside the house, walks back outside. Eyeballs the situation.

Isabel is talking through Seth's open window. Her posture is that of someone with an ignorant sense of courage. Hope strangles the urge to jump up and down, maybe scream.

Isabel returns to the porch, and Seth drives off.

"What did he say?"

"He said it was well within his rights to watch over the house where his kids slept until his whore of a wife got home. I told him he better leave before she did get home because she was out with a badass who'd tear his throat out."

"You told Seth she was out on a date?"

"With that professor guy, right?"

"Dreamboat," Hope confirms.

"I haven't seen him yet!" Isabel complains.

"He wears the coolest necklaces and bracelets."

"Dudes with jewelry, man," Isabel winces. "Lame."

"No, it's cool, though. It's all on these leather straps instead of chains," Hope says. "You'd like his boots, too. Pointy."

"How old is he?"

"A million," Hope says. "But like a hot million. I can't believe you told Seth."

"Who cares?" Isabel says. "He left. Are the boys asleep? Does Regina still have that rum in the kitchen closet?"

The two walk inside and lock the front door behind them.

"I might have had to use it all to clean the soot off the walls," Hope says. "We ran through all the traditional cleaners. In Odenton."

Isabel laughs.

"I love your dad."

Good Friday

Hope is a couple of minutes late for her Friday shift at Coney Castle. It's just Hope and Amy, a skinny girl one year older than Hope with red hair cut into a puffy mullet.

Hope sits on the trunk freezer that holds the chip wheelies and other snack treats. She gets off her perch to eye a gathering out the front window.

One trashy-looking teenage girl wanders toward the triangle that's left of the old giant soft-serve cone. Three guys with her seem to be picking on one skinny kid in cut-off jeans, tube socks, and a Night Ranger tee shirt. The taller of the bullies pushes Tube Socks to the ground, and the boys laugh.

"Uh oh," Hope says. "Redneck riot."

Amy looks.

"That's my sister and my ex-boyfriend."

Hope laughs, embarrassed.

"Oh! Sorry!"

Amy laughs.

"Still, they are about to fight," Hope nods toward the front window.

As they look, Tube Socks pulls nun-chucks out of his back pocket. The two bullies stiffen, visibly freaked.

"No way!" Hope says, excited.

She and Amy move closer to the window for a better look.

"Does your boyfriend have nun-chucks? Dude, who has nun-chucks?! How awesomely white trash is that?!"

"Stop saying that!" Amy laughs.

"Like it isn't?!"

"And he's my ex— exactly because of things like this!"

The three boys outside the window duck and dodge each other. Tube Socks twirls, showing off. The taller of the bullies reaches in as if to take the weapon, but Tube Socks pulls back and releases, hitting the other boy across the face.

The taller bully's head jerks toward Amy and Hope. His body follows.

Blood smacks across the window.

Hope and Amy jump back.

"Aaaahhh!" they yell in unison.

Tube Socks runs off. The shorter bully takes off after him. Hope and Amy put their faces to the window, craning in one direction, trying to see where the tall bully fell. Soon he stands up, holds his tee shirt to his face, and walks silently back across Washington Street.

"Well, it was awesome while it lasted," Hope says.

"Who's cleaning that up?" Amy asks, perturbed.

"Leave it, man. I am doing nothing with blood or other bodily fluids. Obie can figure it out."

They hear the heavy back door open, and they freeze.

"Is it Cara?" Amy whispers.

They make nervous nelly faces at each other until Joy—wearing a hip, oversized teal tee shirt—pokes her head in from the back of the building.

"Just came for my check."

"Dude!" Hope shouts. "You just missed this awesome white trash rumble!"

"What?" she asks, so disappointed.

"These hicks were arguing about monster trucks," Hope begins.

"You don't know that!" Amy laughs, annoyed but amused.

Hope corrects herself.

"Presumably, these hicks were arguing about monster trucks, and Amy's boyfriend—"

"Ex-boyfriend!"

"—pulled out nun-chucks!"

"Lies!" Joy protests.

"I swear it! Look at that blood!"

Hope points to the spatter on the front of the window.

"Gross!" Joy recoils.

"It's like Dawn after her last shift with Cara," Hope says.

"What does that mean?" Amy asks. "Did Cara hit her with nun-chucks?"

"I don't see Cara as the nun-chuck type," Joy muses.

"Switchblade?" Hope proposes.

"Assault rifle," Joy decides.

"What happened?!" Amy asks, impatient.

"Oh my God, you missed such a good day!" Hope begins. She sets herself back on the freezer chest. "Cara just covered Dawn with mustard and catsup."

Joy grabs the condiment bottles and pantomimes.

"She squeezed those bitches like she was putting out a fire. Or one super-sparkle smile."

"Poor Dawn," Amy says.

"Oh my God, it was glorious," Hope counters.

Joy makes herself a shredded chicken sandwich. All three freshen their Coney Castle Styrofoam cups at the pop gun. Then someone raps at the order window behind Amy. It's her sister.

Amy opens up.

"Hey, there's totally a dead guy out by the dumpster," Amy's sister says with a strangely sultry overemphasis on the "s" sound.

Hope looks over, shooting a contemptuous grimace that does not have the impact she'd hoped. The remaining boy reiterates as if the message had been unclear.

"Out back? By the dumpster? There's a dead guy."

"Which one of you is going to clean up that blood?" Amy asks her sister.

"Amy," her sister says dramatically. "I'm serious."

After a long pause with those inside the establishment staring skeptically at those outside, Hope closes the order window.

The shorter bully who'd run after Tube Socks returns to the group out front, and they talk beyond the closed windows, then disappear beside the building.

"I suddenly wish Cara was here," Joy says.

"It's just a lame joke," Hope says. "Or else it's some passed out drunk."

"Yeah," Amy concurs. "It's probably one of the McCoy boys."

"If so, he'll take off with the approach of the mob," Hope predicts.

"Still, maybe Cara will come back," Joy hopes.

"Maybe," Hope says. "She may decide she's light on twenties."

"Like she'd save us," Amy scoffs.

"By accident, she would," Hope says. "She'd take care of the situation, and by doing so, inadvertently save us."

Joy nods her head toward the window.

"Trailer park trio approaches," she says.

Amy hits her in the arm.

"What does Jimmy Slackjaw want now?" Hope wonders, annoyed.

Amy slides the order window up.

"Yep, he's dead," the shorter bully confirms. "I burped in his face and everything."

Amy's sister concurs.

"No seriously, you guys," she says, with again with the s thing. "He's dead."

The group out front looks to the employees to take charge of the situation. Instead, Amy re-closes the order window, and they walk into the back of the building, beyond the sight of customers.

Amy lights a menthol and boosts herself onto a stainless-steel table.

"What if we really are trapped inside a glass building while a corpse rots in the almost-summer sun out in our parking lot?" Hope wonders.

"Surely it isn't so," Joy says.

"You two talk even funnier when you're together than when you're apart," Amy notices. "We should go look."

They eye each other nervously, the situation—or maybe all the sugar—creating a giddy energy among them, like a slumber party watching a scary movie.

They crowd together and slink toward the door. Clinging to each other, Hope in front, they push open the door and peer around it to see how much of the mysterious body they can glimpse.

None.

"And there you have it," Hope says.

"Nothing," Amy says, a bit disappointed.

"Whew!" Joy says.

"Such good news," Hope says. "It's not like he could be somewhere beyond our line of vision and we're just lying to ourselves right now."

"I've always hated you," Joy tells her.

They duck back inside and close the door.

"We should call someone," Joy suggests.

"Obie?" Amy asks.

"No!" Hope objects. "Then he'll just come here."

After a pause, Hope offers, "Dawn?"

"Why Dawn?" Amy wonders.

"We'll lure her over here under the pretense of friendship. She'll walk through the grass right past him."

"She'll just naturally see him," Joy says.

"And she'll just naturally tend to him," Amy agrees.

Hope hands Joy the receiver from the black dial phone hanging on the wall in the back of the Coney Castle.

"Hi, Mrs. Thome," Joy says. "This is Joy Murphy. Is Dawn around?"

Joy frowns. She nods and hangs up.

"She's at synchronized swim lessons."

"Of course, she is!" Hope yells.

"We have to do this ourselves," Amy decides.

They return to the back door, pause, muster their courage, and push it open. The three step out as one teal-wearing, Coney-smelling unit toward the dumpster.

Just past the edge of the rusty metal dumpster, something juts forward. A shoe.

Amy screams.

Hope and Joy scream.

The three stumble, arms flailing, over each other and back inside. Hope turns the deadbolt.

"We should call Cara," Amy recommends. "I feel like she'd know how to handle this."

"She would totally know what to do with a dead body," Joy agrees.

"Bingo," Hope says.

Joy nods, but nobody heads to the phone.

"Go ahead," Hope looks at Amy.

"I'm not calling her. You call her," Amy says.

"Fuck that," Hope says.

"You should call her, Hope," Joy says. "She's friends with you."

"Really?" Hope looks simultaneously terrified and honored.

"She's lying," Amy clarifies. "Everybody likes Joy best."

But Joy isn't calling. The girls can see it on her face.

"Here's what's going to happen," Hope says with calm authority. "Dawn will stop by for her check on her way home from synchronized swimming. She'll see him and tiptoe in closer, hoping to help. He'll reach out with the cold grip of someone returned from the dead."

The three girls look nervously at each other.

"And he'll kill her."

Joy and Amy chuckle uncomfortably.

"We'll hear the screaming and open the door, only to see his limping, tattered rage as he turns his attention to us. We'll slam the door, but he'll begin pounding relentlessly. He'll circle the building. We won't be able to go near the windows. He'll slap wildly at the glass out front, and then all will go silent. Terrified, we'll lock ourselves in the walk-in freezer, but eventually, we'll hear Cara at the back door, wanting to get in for her paycheck. She'll knock to be let in, curse, and bitch about how slow we are. We'll hear her voice trail beside the building, then around front to the windows. Then we'll hear nothing."

Hope pauses dramatically.

"Until the wet thump of her mangled body as it slams against the glass. We'll scream and scream, incapable of saving ourselves as he uses her lifeless corpse to bust through."

After a terrified pause, Amy whispers.

"Let's go back out."

The three head back to the Coney Castle parking lot, this time with a small amount of air between each body. Hope takes the lead but will walk only so far to stay an arm's length ahead of Joy, who keeps a similar distance from Amy.

They inch forward.

There is definitely a whole guy attached to those dirty Nikes. He is on his side, wearing ratty athletic shorts and a green t-shirt. He is freakishly pale. Fishbelly white. Nasty white.

"Is it a McCoy boy?" Hope asks.

"Who can tell? There are so many of them. It could be an older brother. Maybe," Amy ponders.

"Maybe it's the guy who jumped Hannah that time," Hope suggests.

From about 15 feet away, Hope picks up a stone from the lot and throws it in his general direction.

Nothing.

Joy calls to him.

"Excuse me, sir?"

Nothing.

Nun-chucks returns to the scene of the crime, moseying up the driveway.

"Are you going to do something about this?" Amy demands.

He sneers and walks back the way he came.

Amy rolls her eyes.

"Typical."

She picks up some stones. The girls continue calling to the body and tossing stones.

"Hey! Wake up, you bum," Amy yells.

"If you get up, we'll give you free ice cream," Hope offers.

"And a hot dog," Joy continues.

"A footlong!" Amy promises.

Nothing. They throw more stones. They offer more novelty snacks.

"Please get up and go away," Hope pleads.

They huddle desperately together.

"One of us has to go wake him up," Amy says. "At least touch him to see if he's really dead."

Amy looks at Hope expectantly.

"You do it," she says.

"Why is it always me?!" Hope yells.

Amy and Joy stare blankly at her, and she accepts her fate. Hope walks toward the body.

She crouches.

"Hey, heap o' dude," she says quietly, more to herself than anything.

She looks back at the clinging mass of sister/friend behind her, the door to the Coney Castle ajar beyond them, issuing forth waft after waft of Coney stench.

Hope looks back at the dead guy at Coney Castle.

His eyes are open.

"You didn't call the cops, did you?"

"Jesus!" Hope falls to her butt.

The girls scream and run back inside the building, slamming the door as the man pushes himself up and walks wobbly-legged down the alley.

"Is he gone?" Amy asks.

"What direction did he go?" Hope asks.

"Was he a McCoy boy?" Amy wants to know.

"Did he go down the alley?" Hope asks. "We should take the long way home."

"Forget it, pussy," Joy says.

"Don't go yet!" Amy pleads. "Just hang on for like ten minutes to make sure he doesn't come back."

Hope groans.

Joy smacks her.

Eventually, the sisters do leave, taking the same alley as the bum, back toward 93 Second. Behind them, Amy turns off the last light, locks the door, and drags a plastic bag of garbage toward the dumpster. She sets the bag down exactly where the body had been sitting in the sun, waves goodbye to the Murphy girls, then throws open the dumpster lid. Then she lets out a gasp.

A great slamming draws Hope's attention, and she turns to look, but Amy is gone. Hope's attention returns to her sister.

"Shit, I forgot the chicken sandwiches," Hope groans.

"You going to Regina's?" Joy asks her.
"Yep," Hope confirms.

"She won't eat chicken today," Joy reminds her. "Good Friday."

Hope slaps herself on the forehead. Then points to her sister.

"You did!" she shakes her head. "Sinner."

They walk down the darkening alley.

"Regina went out last night," Hope says mysteriously.

"Out out?" Joy asks.

"Like a date."

"Who with?" Joy asks.

"This dreamy outsider guy," Hope says. "He's like European or something."

"Nice."

"His teeth are crooked in the best way," she says. "His lips are so full…"

"Bee stung lips," Joy says.

"It makes you just want to bite them."

Joy laughs.

"He was at that party I crashed where the blonde lady was mad about my vampire dreams," Hope says. She pauses, recalling something. "I think he was there when that guy rear-ended me and smashed up the car, too."

"I knew it!" Joy yells.

"I didn't say it didn't happen. I just didn't say it did. And then Dad came up with his own story."

"And Regina's boyfriend was there?" Joy asks.

"I think so," Hope realizes. "I was kind of woozy, but nobody talks like him."

"How does he talk?"

"I don't know," Hope says. "Not like Odenton. And he dresses—boots, but not cowboy boots; jeans, but not townie jeans. Like a hip European Johnny Cash with these big full lips and gorgeous crooked teeth. Are you hanging out with the choir kids tonight?"

Joy nods.

"Try not to wreck another car."

The two split up on Second Avenue. Joy walks into 93, Hope into 95, next door.

The Oliver family is seated in the kitchen, digging into plates of spaghetti.

"Look who's here!" Regina smiles.

Hope plops into Seth's long-empty chair.

"Do you want a plate?" Regina asks.

Before Hope can decide, they hear a knock.

"We're eating!" Scott yells toward the front door.

"Scott!" Regina laughs and hushes.

Isabel lets herself in.

"Hello, Olivers!" she says sweetly.

"Well, hello there, stranger," Regina says. "Do you want some spaghetti?"

"Oh, no thanks," Isabel responds. "Just coming for Hope."

"Are we doing something?" Hope asks.

"Yes," Isabel tells her.

"Without a car?"

"We have a ride."

Pause.

"Oh, go ahead," Regina says to Hope, and then to Isabel, "She doesn't want the spaghetti anyway. It has vegetables in the sauce."

"Thanks, peach!" Hope says, while Scott simultaneously whines, "Why do I have to eat it, then?!"

Hope pushes away from the table, and she and Isabel walk out the front door.

"See ya, Oliver, Oliver, Oliver!" Isabel shouts behind her.

"Where are we going?" Hope asks.

"Party out at Bermans."

They let the screen door slam behind them.

"JP will be out there."

"Tragic," Hope says. "You are tragic."

Isabel ignores her. They cross the Oliver front yard heading toward the Murphy house.

"How are we getting out there?"

"That girl you work with," Isabel says nonchalantly. "Cara."

Hope stops walking.

"I'm sorry?" Hope says, almost laughing.

"Come again?" Isabel responds.

"We're not really going to a party with Cara Romig," Hope says more than she asks.

They stand, facing each other under the lengthening shadow of a still-naked maple branch.

"Why not?" Isabel responds, half ignoring her. "She has a car. You don't."

Isabel starts back toward Hope's house.

"Why don't you get a fucking car?" Hope complains, chasing after her.

"If I had a boyfriend, I wouldn't need a car."

"JP Young?" Hope grimaces. "Gross. Where's she picking us up? She's not coming to my house, is she?"

"Why not?"

The two continue walking through the Murphy front yard and toward the Gehrigs'. Over her shoulder, Hope notices Honey drag a big outdoor garbage can to the side of her house. She's pulling something from the floor of the storage closet.

Hope stops.

Dead cats. Limp little bodies, smashed heads.

Honey looks up at Hope, then away. Before Isabel notices, Hope grabs her by the arm and pulls her quickly to the sidewalk.

"Why can't Cara pick us up here?" Isabel asks.

Hope shakes the image of the cats from her head.

"Oh, Mom's nurse is like religious," Hope says.

"Not Catholic?" Isabel confirms.

"No, some flavor of Protestant," Hope says. "Like a no-dancing, no-drinking zealot type. She thinks Cara Romig is a witch."

"Oh my god, Odenton is so dumb."

They're all the way to the Fabrizios' by this point. Hope looks at the screened-in porch. She thinks of Bloody Fingers and of Honey Gehrig's cats. She imagines Howdy dragging himself down the enclosed apartment stairs, maddened by echoey mews, his bloody fingers scraping each step in front of him.

"You should just get a Catholic nurse," Isabel says.

"That's clearly the answer," Hope deadpans. "They send whoever they send."

"I should be your mom's nurse," Isabel says.

"They like you better than me already."

They walk along silently past the Cassidy house. Isabel's is within eyeshot.

"They'd like you better if you were in the choir, like Joy. Or if you played sports."

"Seventeen might be late to develop hand-eye coordination."

"Almost eighteen!" Isabel cheers.

The two girls walk silently until they get to Isabel's front porch.

"Hey, Ray Ray." Hope waves during his indecipherable response, and the pair takes a seat on the porch steps to wait for Cara.

"Where are we going, again?" Hope asks.

"A party."

A white Aries K car slows to a stop, and Hope and Isabel hop up to join Cara. They drive back the way they came, and Hope ducks as they pass the Murphy house, even though she knows no one will be looking. The maple tree birds have moved to Regina's house, congregating like a dark, living seam running down the center of her roof.

One bird lifts, then glides toward the car, dipping back up right in front of the windshield. The others follow. Cara hits the brakes.

"What is the deal with these birds?" she yells, both impressed and annoyed. "It's like they're trained!"

Hope says nothing, still looking back at her own front door just in case. The birds finish their dance, and she turns to see the whole chorus line follow-the-leader to the Stimmells' barn. Hope stares as they clutch the roof and eaves.

"That's where that guy murdered Katrina McCoy," Cara announces as if guiding some kind of morbid tour. Isabel and Hope share a glance. They know.

"I bet if they tore that barn down, they'd find Joannie Fabrizio's body," Cara guesses. "He probably buried it under the floorboards somewhere."

Cara hits the gas, and they head up Second Avenue toward the edge of town.

"One stop first," Cara says to her passengers.

She takes a left, snakes through the neighborhood toward the railroad tracks, and halts in front of the McCoy house. Cara grabs her oversized faux-suede handbag and opens her door.

"You coming?"

"We're good here," from the back seat.

Hope and Isabel sink uncomfortably into seats as Cara mounts the McCoy porch and knocks. Katrina's older sister Renee—Katrina used to call her NayNay; she terrified Hope and Isabel in grade school—opens the door. Hope doesn't find her scary anymore, just sad. NayNay calls behind her, and Katrina's younger brother Curtis comes out.

Like all of Katrina's brothers, Curtis is trouble. He just hasn't had the chance to really prove himself yet. The McCoy kids have never really been right, but they have been full-bore wrong since Katrina died. You would think the town sympathy would have lasted, but the more Odenton turned Katrina into a defenseless angel, the more they judged her parents and the more her siblings suffered by comparison. Six years later, and it's like the wound never healed. It only festered.

Many people assume one or more of Katrina's older brothers actually killed her, but they'd never been investigated. Gaietto liked Eric Stimmel for the crime, and Eric had no one to corroborate his story that he was in bed. That was that.

Curtis McCoy is staring into the car.

Hope gets nervous that a McCoy boy is about to get into the car and ride to the party with them. Curtis McCoy would have to sit in the back seat with her. The longer he stares, the more Hope wants to open the door and walk home before it's too late.

Then Cara hands NayNay a clear plastic bag and leaves, no McCoys in tow.

The car heads back toward the edge of town. Cara takes a left on what feels to Hope like any random rural route and turns up the Iron Maiden.

"I hear there's a coven out here," Cara tells them.

"Yeah?" Isabel feigns interest.

"There's totally not," from the back seat. "Like not here, not anywhere. Total bullshit. Paranoid, ignorant fucking bullshit."

"Oh, right!" Cara disagrees. "Out in Willard, their basketball team was #1 in the state. Tiny little Willard. They were undefeated. Then there was that murder—a satanic ritual—and they lost their next game."

"And you think somebody sacrificed a human life over high school basketball?" Hope scoffs.

"It is rural Ohio," Isabel points out.

It's not entirely dark yet when the car stops at a big brick house surrounded by nothing: empty fields, no barn, no telephone wires, nothing. What Hope hates the most about the country is the lack of streetlights.

The three girls head inside. Hope recognizes two older boys—probably home for Easter break: Brad and Cody Peabody. Like all OLPH students, Hope had a flaming crush on Cody Peabody in fourth grade.

Lee Green, from the grade behind Hope and Isabel, is also there with his Freshman brother, Johnny.

Not what Hope had expected. She figured they'd fall into a huge sprawl of kids, all of them outside, most of them in line for a keg hidden in a barn. Def Leppard would blare from somebody's boom box, and if you got too far from that music source, somebody else would be playing Poison. She'd expected an outdoor event. More people. Girls.

"This isn't the party," Isabel whispers. "It's another stop-off. I see now why we don't want to ride with Cara. Sorry!"

Cara pulls a plastic baggie out of her purse, and Brad shouts, "Hey Howdy, they're here."

Howdy Noonan strolls out of the bathroom and into the living room, where everyone stands awkwardly. Cara approaches Howdy Noonan, and Hope realizes she just wants to leave. She turns to find Isabel when Cody Peabody and the Green brothers walk toward her, making a semicircle around Hope, smiling.

"Can I smoke in here?" she asks.

They say nothing but keep walking even when they're too close to her, so she backs up into a small room with a coat rack.

"Where's your sister?" Brad asks her.

"She's at another party," Hope says. She pulls a pack of Marlboro Lights from her back pocket. The boys are still moving slowly in her direction, but lighting the cigarette stops them.

Hope smiles uncomfortably.

They smile.

Four sets of shoulders block most of the light from the main room. Hope takes in the space she's in—what is it, a coat room? Storage? She backs another step and feels the washer/drier behind her.

She's reminded of a song from when she was little.

Come be with me
Come play with me
We'll go, you'll see

Secret place, you and me
Chickadee

She gives the song some space in her head and looks contemplatively at the young men crowding the entrance to this small room.

"You guys hanging' out here?" It's more of an annoyed statement than a question. "Looks like a rockin' time."

"Why are you wearing that sweater?" Brad asks her. "It's hot."

"Wouldn't you be more comfortable if you took it off?" Lee Green asks. His younger brother doesn't say anything, just smiles. The smile is ill-fitting. It seems genuine, not creepy, not douchy. Nervous. Sorry.

"Come on," Brad asks. "We're all friends."

"Take it off," Cody orders. "Quit playing."

Hope pulls at the crumpled pack of smokes. She sets her lighter on top of the dryer, next to an assortment of aerosol starches, anti-static sprays, and pre-wash cleaners.

"Well?" Brad asks again.

She fingers the lighter.

"I'm good," she says.

The three boys look at each other. Brad eyeballs Lee Green and motions toward Hope.

She remembers being chased by a bird under the neighbor's porch. How did she get out of that? She wishes Joy were here.

Hope takes a drag, lays her hand on the aerosol can, wobbles it back and forth.

The lights in the next room flicker. Suddenly birds are cawing loudly from outside, flapping and crashing, their shadows creating a ruckus in the room. But from where? Hope can't find a window.

When the lights stabilize, a shadow reaches from somewhere behind Hope. It darkens the floor around her and the half of her body leaning on the dryer.

Lee Green looks at the two older boys as if for direction.

"You guys have like an ashtray or anything?" Hope asks.

"Yeah, actually, you probably shouldn't smoke in here," Lee Green answers.

"Yeah," Brad says. "You'll get them in trouble."

"Well, I guess I'll wait for Isabel and Cara out front."

She ashes on the floor, pushes past the boys, and walks back through the living room to the front door and the porch.

By the time Cara and Isabel join her and the trio gets on the road to the party, Hope's weary of being out. She'd rather just go home and now realizes that, with Scary Cara Romig at the wheel, she will have no control over the night at all.

They land at a farmhouse Hope vaguely recognizes. It's far enough from the city to have well water and use a generator for outdoor lights. Cara parks, and the three head toward party noise. Isabel points to a car across the road.

"Is that Seth Oliver's muscle car?"

Hope squints. It's too dark to tell.

"Is he here for the sweet teen poontang?" Cara laughs.

Hope winces.

"His parents live one farm over," Hope says. "I dropped the boys off there once. He's staying there until they come back up from Florida."

"Is that where he's hiding out?" Cara laughs wickedly, and the three head toward the party.

Christmas lights are strung from the barn to the back door, although you're not allowed inside the house except to pee. When Hope meanders toward the back door, a young man with a flat-top blocks her way.

"You need to piss?"

"What?" she asks him, startled.

"You can only come in to use the toilet," he says, almost friendly.

"Ah," Hope says and turns back to the party.

"Keg's in the barn," he tells her.

Hope makes her way to the keg, fills a cup as Def Leppard buzzes through the barn, and walks to the tractor she's been eyeing while standing in line. With her free hand and sturdy brown boots, she climbs the tire treads, then perches atop for a drink and a better view of the party.

"Hey," she calls down to two girls who stop to talk at the nose of the tractor. They look up. "Whose party is this?"

"Roberta Berman's," the blonder of the two says. Her friend points to a petite brunette laughing near the beer pong table.

Hope looks around. She can't see Isabel. She can't see Cara. There are no Calvary kids within eyeshot. She thinks she vaguely recognizes one or two boys, but she hardly knows them well enough to ask them for a ride back to town.

She sits, drinks her beer, and hopes nobody will steal her spot when she eventually jumps down for a refill.

No one does, so she refills a few times and waits for her friend. A large figure begins a slow but clear path toward her from the other side of the keg line. She recognizes him: Howdy Noonan. Again.

Sad, that—when twentysomethings have nothing better to do than crash a high school party. He stops at her feet. Looks up.

"Hey," he says.

Hope half-smiles.

"I mean, howdy neighbor," he corrects himself.

Hope raises her eyebrows and nods.

"Your sister here?"

"Nope."

"How old are you now?" he asks.

"Eighteen Sunday," she responds, looking over his head to find anyone—just anyone—at this party she knows well enough to give her an excuse to drop down and run off.

"So, underage today..."

She looks at him and grimaces just as she spies Mickey Wright leaving the house's back door with Strawberry Carl.

"Mickey!" she hollers and leaps to the ground.

She runs toward the house. Mickey looks confused. Or high.

"Hey," she says.

"Yeah…" he smiles. "This is my buddy Strawberry."

"Dude, I know her," Strawberry laughs. "Isabel here?"

"She is, but I haven't seen her since we got here. I think she was looking for J.P. Young."

"Dude," Strawberry says, disappointed.

"Too right," Hope responds.

"Hey, remember that time J.P. Young's dad nabbed you from the back of my truck?" Strawberry laughs.

"No. I don't remember that at all."

"Really?" Strawberry asks earnestly.

"Dude," Hope smacks him in the head. "It was three days ago."

"Right. So, sorry for bailing on you and everything," Strawberry says.

"Hey, Isabel!!" Mickey Wright calls loudly.

She's exiting the barn with Cara, who stops to talk to a small group, digging in her bag as she does.

"Isabel!" Strawberry calls with him.

Hope is set to join the third call when Isabel smiles and waves, begins walking toward the threesome. J.P. Young—not good looking, not lean, not especially smart or interesting, so what is the deal anyway?—steps from the shadows where Isabel had been standing and moves toward her, but she ignores him.

"Hey!" she says. "What's up?"

A clearly stoned Strawberry crumples next to Mickey before offering Isabel a strangely formal handshake. She looks confused but shakes his hand.

"Dude, Howdy Noonan was talking to me," Hope tells her, clearly annoyed.

"Howdy Noonan?" Strawberry asks. "Dude, he'll like burn you at the stake or something."

"Is he a witch?" Mickey asks and laughs. "I mean, a Merlin?"

More giggling.

"Warlock," Isabel corrects him, and they all laugh.

"Shut up," Hope says, friendly but firm.

Mickey's looking out into the plowed, mainly empty field.

"I bet they have pot out there."

"Oh my God, don't be stupid," Hope says.

"No, but what's that big thing?" Isabel points. "Like a scarecrow or something?"

"Ooo, creepy!" Strawberry smiles. "Let's check it!"

He pulls on Isabel's arm and runs toward the field. The rest semi-reluctantly follow. The field is very dark. They stumble in the ruts between rows and have to keep their eyes on their feet.

"This is the worst," Mickey says.

"At least it's not hot," Strawberry offers. "It used to be hot, remember, friends?"

Mickey stumbles.

"I don't want to play anymore."

"It'd be easier if they offered us a piggyback ride," Strawberry says.

Hope and Isabel look at each other, bemused and confused.

Strawberry loses energy and drops to his back in the field. Isabel pulls him by the arm, but he doesn't budge.

"We could race," Mickey says. "Piggyback race."

"We'd carry you?" Hope asks, just to clarify. She makes a crumple-nosed 'let's not' face at Isabel, but it's too dark to see.

"OK," Isabel decides, looking at Strawberry. "I'll take you. Get up."

"Right," Hope says, looking at Mickey, who is all smiles.

"Don't drop me. I'm fragile," he says. Hope plants her feet in two ruts and braces for Mickey.

"Dude, you're so heavy!" she complains.

"Ha, fatty!" Strawberry taunts.

"Don't hurt my feelings," Mickey says.

"You guys ready?" Hope asks. Isabel and Strawberry clearly are not, so she puts Mickey down.

"OK, OK, OK," Strawberry says. "For real."

He hops on Isabel's back as Mickey re-mounts, and the two girls begin a labored run. Isabel takes an easy lead, and Mickey complains in Hope's ear.

"Let's not be losers, eh?"

Strawberry slides off Isabel's back, and while they work that out, Hope and Mickey pass them.

The whole affair lasts maybe 30 feet before Hope's foot twists in the plowed field, and she falls, smacking her knee on some kind of root. Mickey lands easily on his feet, but Hope is down.

"We won!" Mickey declares. "We are gimp but victorious!"

Hope laughs from the ground, but Isabel and Strawberry are silent. Mickey turns around.

Immediately behind Hope loom three big, crookedly planted crosses.

"Man…" Strawberry says, creeped out.

Hope looks up.

"Is that like for Easter, or are they always there?" Isabel asks.

"Might be for scarecrows?" Mickey says. "Maybe somebody took them down for the season?"

"Are scarecrows seasonal?" Hope asks, struggling to get back to her feet.

"I don't know, man," Mickey admits. "I'm from the Avenues. You OK?"

"I'm good," Hope says, limping a little.

"Beer will help heal ya," Mickey offers.

"To beer!" Isabel shouts as they make their way back to the party. Hope peers over her shoulder from time to time, relieved when distance and darkness blot out the crosses.

Mickey's right. Beer helps. But by the time Isabel and Strawberry are kissing, Hope is ready to bail.

"Is there any chance you can drive me back to the Avenues?" she asks Mickey when he returns from the barn. He smiles, points to a zip lock baggie hidden in his jeans pocket.

"Not a problem! Got what I came for. Let's hit it."

Blue and red lights flash across Mickey's face.

The sheriff.

Mickey bolts, as do other partygoers. All scatter into the surrounding empty fields, including Isabel. Hope hobbles after, but it's no use.

This feels familiar.

About to resign herself to her jailbird destiny, she sees Strawberry double back for her.

"I won't leave you behind again!" he shouts. He reaches Hope, and they three-leg it back to his truck.

Holy Saturday

Hope wakes up late. She limps down the hall—Joy's already gone, her room's empty—then down the stairs.

"Dude!" she says, surprised to see Bridget at the bottom of the steps. "Why are you here?"

Hope crosses the room and kisses her mom on the head.

"I smell nasty," she warns.

Mrs. Murphy almost looks perky. Happy to see Bridget.

"What do you have planned today?" Bridget asks.

"Hangin' next door, mostly. Cleaning the walls again, then probably painting them. What are you doing here?"

"I'm here to help Sheriff Gaietto develop a kind of profile of cultists," Bridget explains.

"Oh my God," Hope complains. "Don't freak Mom out with this."

Mrs. Murphy looks right at Hope and shakes her head as if to say, I'm not buying any of it.

"Innocent people are less likely to be harassed if the police know what to look for," Bridget says. "They do tend to fit a pattern."

"Anybody different," Hope dismisses her. "He's all 'it was almost a full moon' and 'we're just a week away from an important solstice.' I mean, he just pulls dumbassedness from horror movies, combines werewolf stuff with witch stuff. He can't even keep his horror movie mythology straight."

"There must be something up if he asked me to drive down here, though," Bridget says. "He was pretty cryptic."

"How come it's never just the stepdad? The boyfriend?" Hope asks. "Like in every other normal town."

Bridget looks at her sister.

"Are you limping?"

"Nope. Hey," Hope redirects, "Are my CDs and posters safe with you here?"

"It's a little alarming, actually. You basically fit the profile with your movies, tee-shirts, and that guy on his knees in a ring of fire."

"Billy Idol," Hope clarifies. "Totally harmless." She kisses her mom's cheek and addresses her warmly. "Taking my Satan movie and going to Regina's."

Mrs. Murphy pats Hope's free hand.

"Brush your teeth first," Bridget says.

Hope covers her mouth, nods, and complies.

On the front porch, Hope pivots left, walks between her house and her neighbor's. Something flutters and disappears from the top of Regina's roof. Hope looks, trips on her neighbor's porch step and looks back toward where she's going.

She walks in without ringing the bell.

Scott looks up from his bucket of Legos.

"Hope's here!" he yells to anyone and no one, then begins digging again for the elusive yellow brick.

Hope walks into the kitchen, where Regina is cleaning up breakfast dishes. The room is very bright without the curtains. It really draws attention to the soot Hope missed.

"Hey there!" Regina says. Hope opens the refrigerator. "Lucky for you, we've already been to the store. Plenty of diet Coke."

Hope helps herself.

"I'm surprised to see you," Regina says, hanging the damp dishtowel over a drawer pull. "Didn't I see Bridget's car?"

"She's sitting with Mom," Hope says. "She's in town for some Gaietto clown show."

"You'll go back and sit with your mom when she leaves?" Regina asks.

"I guess so. Nobody specified, but I didn't see Joy at home. No idea where she is."

"That's what happens when you sleep until noon," Regina points out. "People just get on with their days. You're in time to go with us to buy some paint."

"Do you know what I feel like eating?" Hope asks. "Honeycombs."

"With Diet Coke?" Regina grimaces.

"Someone's at the door," Nicholas announces from his book-reading perch on the stairs.

Hope turns—Sheriff Gaietto.

"Regina," she loud-whispers.

"What is it?" Regina comically loud-whispers back.

"Police action."

They exchange a glance.

"Use the back door," Regia recommends.

"Roger that."

Hope ducks out the back door, cuts through her own backyard, and heads into the Murphy kitchen. She can't see her mom dozing in the blue chair anymore and wonders fleetingly where she went. Having left her beverage at Regina's, Hope opens the refrigerator door looking for a diet Pepsi.

Bridget pokes her head in.

"I'm so glad you're home," she says. "Where's Joy?"

"Dunno."

"The sheriff just went next door to get you."

"You sent the sheriff after me?!"

"I have something to talk about with you two," Bridget admits.

"What?"

"I'd rather wait and tell you and Joy together."

"Dude, I'm going back to bed," Hope says. "Spill it now, and I can tell Joy."

"They found a body in the dumpster at Coney Castle," Bridget says quickly.

"What? No, no," Hope laughs. "We thought this guy was dead out by the dumpster, but it turns out he was just passed out. It was fine."

"Who was it?" Bridget demands. "We should get the sheriff back over here."

"No, he was fine. I don't know who he was. Some McCoy boy, maybe. Or just some drunky, but he was fine. We woke him up, and he left."

"Were you working with someone named Amy?" Bridget asks.

"Yeah, Amy, Joy, and me," Hope says. "Well, Joy wasn't working—she came by to get her check—but it was the three of us there when the guy was there."

Bridget stops her, holds her hand. Hope stiffens.

"That's who they found," Bridget says quietly. "Someone named Amy."

Hope stares at her, not entirely grasping what she said.

"I guess the neighbors behind Coney Castle use that dumpster sometimes, and the mom—" she starts.

"Dawn's mom," Hope realizes.

"Maybe. She took some bags over, and when she threw them in, she saw your friend."

"Inside the dumpster?!" Hope yells, horrified. Suddenly dizzy, she sits on the floor in front of the refrigerator door and stares bewildered between her shoes.

"I'm so sorry, chickadee," Bridget tells her. "You stay put. I'm going to go out front to see if the sheriff is still around; let him know you were there and you saw someone suspicious."

Hope sits on the floor for what feels like a long time when Joy comes in through the back door.

She looks at Hope on the floor.

"What's going on, floor sitter?" she asks.

"Amy from work is dead. Dawn's mom found her inside the dumpster."

"What?!" Joy yells. "Are you joking?!"

Joy sits next to Hope on the floor. It's not very clean, the floor. Hope looks at a trail of dried coffee from the stove to the sink, realizes she better wash it before Hannah comes tomorrow.

"Is Bridget here? Her car's out front," Joy asks.

"She went to get Gaietto so we can tell him about that passed-out guy."

"Oh, yeah," Joy remembers. "Man, I cannot believe…that is so awful. You think it was that guy? Like hiding inside the dumpster or something?"

"I feel like we'd have noticed, maybe."

"Somebody had to tell us about him when he was outside the dumpster," Joy reminds her. "We wouldn't have noticed him otherwise."

"Who'd get inside a dumpster?" Hope grimaces.

"That guy would," Joy says.

"I cannot fucking believe this," Hope says flatly.

"Poor Amy," Joy says, just as flatly.

When Bridget returns, she's clearly glad to see Joy.

"Oh, my loves. All safe."

She squeezes between the two on the floor, puts an arm around both, and hugs.

"It's worse than we think," Bridget says. "I guess there were more bodies."

"Fuck!" Hope yells.

Bridget elbows her and throws a glance in the direction of the other room. The three stand and quietly walk out the back door.

"Who?" Joy asks.

"He didn't say," Bridget admits as the three turn to walk between the Murphy and Oliver houses toward the front yard. "But I got really worried that you weren't back yet."

She hugs Joy.

"I'm fine," Joy says stiffly.

Bridget pulls Hope into the hug.

"Dude, we're fine," Hope says, also stiffly.

"Where is Dad?" Joy asks.

"He has a table," Bridget explains. "He said Hannah would want it, so he drove it up to them, and he'll come back tomorrow with them for Easter."

They can see Gaietto standing near his car on Second Avenue. Bridget waves to get the sheriff's attention.

"He has a table," Joy repeats.

"It's probably out of somebody's basement," Hope says.

"I'm sure Hannah is pleased," Joy deadpans.

"Be nice," Bridget says. "Dad's having a hard time."

The three take seats on the porch steps. They sit quietly as Sheriff Gaietto makes his way to them.

"Darryl, Hope and Joy say there was a suspicious man at Coney Castle yesterday. The man was passed out in front of the dumpster where the body was found."

"Interesting," he says. He looks at Hope. "You always seem nearby to disaster, don't you?"

"Odenton's small," Joy tells him. "Everybody is nearby."

"They thought it might be a McCoy," Bridget says.

"I would expect you to think that," Gaietto nods knowingly. "But the culprit is rarely the one you'd expect."

"Statistically untrue," Joy says.

"Untrue?" Gaietto asks. "Satan is the father of lies."

Hope and Joy look at each other.

"What?" Hope asks.

Gaietto smiles.

"Not for me to say, girl," he inhales deeply. "It's for me to put on the full armor of God and take my stand against the devil's schemes."

Gaietto swaggers toward his patrol car, and the three sisters share an uneasy glance.

"Well, I feel safer," Joy deadpans.

Bridget tells her sisters, "I think you two need to stick around. It'll make me too nervous if you're not here. But can you guys keep the music down, just keep it quiet, so Mom doesn't wake up?"

"No," Joy says. "But we can go make noise at Regina's."

As they walk up Regina's front porch steps, Hope spies Nicholas through the screen door.

"Hey, buddy!"

Nicholas opens the door.

"Want to build some Legos?" he asks the girls.

"Do I ever!" Joy responds.

Joy honestly just really loves Legos.

After a few minutes, Regina enters the kitchen from the garage with tarps. She walks to the living room and notices the girls with minimal surprise.

"Are you guys staying to help or just to play?" Regina wonders.

They abandon the boys to their blocks and follow Regina into the kitchen.

"They found this girl we work with dead in the dumpster at Coney Castle."

"What?!" Regina yells.

Joy nods solemnly.

"It's sad," Joy adds. "She was really nice."

Regina squeezes Joy's arm supportively.

"Who was it?"

"Amy – I don't actually know her last name," Hope says. "But she and her sister lived on Washington somewhere. The sister and a bunch of friends were at work yesterday causing a ruckus, and there was this guy passed out behind the dumpster. Then we left, and somebody killed her."

Regina holds her hand to her mouth. She looks around her charred kitchen. Hope follows her eyes and winces with shame.

"You know what?" Regina begins wearily. "Let's just take care of this another day."

"I am so sorry," Hope says and means it.

Joy wanders back into the living and sinks into the corner of the couch, piecing together some secret Lego project she won't tell the others about. The boys take their stacks of blocks to the couch cushion next to her, kneeling on the floor and losing many blocks between cushions. Hope lies deep in the shag below them, lazily clicking blocks together in random fashion.

Regina looks out the window. Bridget and the sheriff are still on the Murphy front lawn.

"I wonder if one of you should go check on your mom. I don't know how long he's kept Bridget out there."

"The nurse is there," Joy reminds her.

"I'll go," Hope says, limping out the front door, across the lawns and into 93 Second.

She catches the attention of the two on the sidewalk as she moves inside the house.

"What are they doing?" Joy asks Regina.

"Looks like they're following Hope," she says.

"They can't go in the house," Joy states matter-of-factly.

"I don't think Bridget would let him in," Regina begins, but she's too late. Joy is on the move.

"Hey," Joy shouts as she makes her way home. "Don't go in there."

The sheriff looks toward the smallest of the Murphy girls with a bemused grin.

"Oh, no? And why not?"

"Because you're not fucking invited." Joy is not messing around.

"We don't want you to disturb our mom," Bridget reminds him from the sidewalk.

Sheriff Gaietto collects himself.

"Of course," he says. "Can you fetch your twin for me, please?"

"No," Joy responds.

"Joy!" Bridget says, surprised. And then to Gaietto, "I'll get her."

As Bridget and Hope emerge from the Murphy house, Joy moves across the yard toward her sisters. Gaietto clears his throat.

"More leads than we can follow at this point," he says to no one in particular. "Two other bodies were identified. Well, we knew who they were from the start. But the farmer didn't know them, so we were able to keep it quiet until their parents were informed."

"Oh, no," Bridget says. "They were young kids, too?"

"Surprised us," Gaietto says. "Weren't what we expected to find when we got the call. But then again, when you play with fire and all."

"What are you talking about?" Hope asks, more bothered by his tone than curious.

"Jerry Berman found them out there. Saw scarecrows out in his field. He doesn't have any scarecrows, you know. Says the sight made his stomach sick. Ran out without saying anything because he didn't want his family to notice, hoping the whole time it wasn't what he was afraid of."

Darryl Gaietto pauses dramatically.

"Thought the one in the middle was a dog until he got close up," he says. "A goat."

Hope reflexively covers her mouth with her hand.

"A goat planted in the middle, like our Lord," Gaietto says. "With a young girl on either side."

Another dramatic pause.

"Looks like Cara Romig's crowd finally turned on her."

"Oh, no…" Bridget murmurs. "You two knew her, too, didn't you?" Bridget reaches around and brings both of her sisters in close to her. She kisses Joy's head, then Hope's. "I'm so sorry."

Hope stares in disbelief.

"Oh, Hope knows her. Maybe better than she lets on. Pretty sure you knew them both," Sheriff Gaietto says, struggling against the hint of a smile.

"Oh, no…" Bridget says again.

"Do you know, was Isabel McCaully mixed up in anything dark?"

Everything gets bleary for Hope, just bright colors bleeding together, sounds crashing against her head. Bridget's squeezing her and crying. Joy stands stiffly on the other side, her head hung.

Hope sucks air. She pushes her sister off of her, staggers into the yard.

Gaietto catches her arm. She pulls away. The noise is ugly: deep, throaty barking and high-pitched cackling and cawing. She sits on the ground, stares ahead.

A dog in the middle. Two birds on either side. A big black bird and a little white bird.

Sheriff Gaietto is yelling, pointing toward Hope. Bridget stands in front of him, her back to Hope.

"She needs some time to digest this, Darryl," Bridget says firmly.

"There is no time," he yells. "I'm tired of this dance with the Murphys."

He advances on Hope.

Joy's having none of it. She stands directly in his path, digs her heels into the earth of the Murphy front yard, and throws her hands out in front of her. She pushes him back into Bridget.

"We want a lawyer right now before she talks to you," Joy says.

"So, she has something to hide?" he smiles drily.

"Where were you last night?" Joy asks. "How do we know you didn't do it, you creepy old fat pervy small-town cop?

"Joy!" Bridget reacts without thinking.

"Did anything like this ever, ever happen in Odenton before you came here? You are the reason for this. You are to blame."

The sheriff shifts uncomfortably from foot to foot.

"Stay away from her," Joy says again.

She turns, helps her twin to her feet, and together they walk to Regina's house.

"Why is Hope crying?" Scott whispers to his mother.

Hope walks past him and curls up on the living room couch. Joy follows, lifts Hope's head and sets it in her lap.

Regina squeezes in under Hope's legs, and the boys climb up and onto their mom's lap. The whole group exhales, holds hands, closes their eyes, and lets their closeness try to keep them safe.

By the time Scott grows antsy, there's movement on the porch. Regina wriggles free and opens the front door. Bridget is crying.

"They need to come home," she whispers.

Regina hugs her, and Bridget holds tight for a beat longer than expected. The two walk in together.

"Hope and Joy, you need to come home. Right now."

"Boys, come on," Regina gently commands, grabbing a couple of coloring books and some crayons. "Let's go over to the Murphys' house."

Like confused, weary zombies, the four on the couch follow.

Next door, Regina ushers the boys quietly into the kitchen, and the three sisters stand near Maureen Murphy's bed. They don't talk to each other. Hope and Joy stare, confused. There is a nurse and another person—a doctor?—in the room with them, standing at a polite distance. Bridget sits on the corner of the bed nearest her mother's head and tells her, crying softly, that it's time. That her parents and her brother are waiting for her.

Hope rouses from her stupor. She looks at Joy, whose sob catches as she takes her mother's hand.

Hope stands at the foot of the bed. Her cheap drug store makeup is already streaked from tears, but her eyes are dry for the moment. Her mom takes a breath. It sounds like a coffee percolator. Then silence. Hope's holding her breath, too, so she feels how long before her mom takes another breath. Hope gets dizzy. Her face is warm and wet, and she realizes she's crying again. Mrs. Murphy takes another loud, labored breath. Later, another. And then, no more.

The front door opens without a knock, and Regina pokes her head around to limit any interruption. She wipes her eyes and sees Sheriff Gaietto inside the Murphys' front door. He's smirking.

She walks with purpose toward him, puts her hand out in front of her, and pushes him back onto the front porch.

"I swear to god, Darryl Gaietto, if you harass these girls while Mrs. Murphy is still in this house, I will make you regret the day you ever decided to run for Sheriff of Odenton."

He stumbles.

"Is she—"

"If not now, soon," Regina softens. "Please go."

Regina continues to answer the Murphy door as the afternoon moves to evening. She answers the phone, takes covered dishes from concerned neighbors, makes coffee, and hugs Murphy girls, all while her sons keep busy and try to stay quiet with crayons at the kitchen table.

Eventually, eyeing Hope and Joy slouched on the couch, she suggests, "Why don't you two go next door for a little while? Get away for a bit? I'll send the boys for you when Hannah and your dad get here."

"We want to go!" the boys yell from the kitchen.

"It's ok," Joy says. "They can come."

Next door, Joy dumps a big puzzle on the floor for the boys and then sits on the couch beyond her sister's feet.

There's a long, unbroken silence. Then Joy gets up and turns on the TV. She pats Nicholas on the head, sits close to her sister and whispers.

"Did you go to that party out at Bermans' farm?"

Hope nods.

"You and Isabel didn't go home together?"

"Cops came. I came home with Strawberry," Hope says wearily. "Isabel disappeared with Cara."

"Cara was with you?"

Joy's having a tough time keeping it to a whisper. She turns up the TV.

"Where did they go?" Joy asks her.

"In that field where they found them." Hope sobs quietly. "Between Bermans' and Regina's in-laws'."

"Where Seth lives?" Joy whispers.

Hope nods.

There's another long quiet spell. Joy leans in to whisper very quietly.

"Do you think Seth did it?"

"No!" Hope reacts. Then more quietly, "Like he's a witch now?"

"No, he's just an asshole," Joy says.

Joy looks sympathetically at her sister, then sighs.

"I don't want you to think about it, but think about it. In all the time they've cried Satan in this town, has anybody ever done anything so elaborate? It's basically gift-wrapped."

"Maybe Gaietto did it," Hope offers weakly.

"But why would he kill them?" Joy asks.

"Why would Seth?" Hope whispers.

Scott tosses puzzle pieces around in frustration, but Nicholas quietly listens as he works.

"What if Isabel and Cara ran over to Seth's parents house to keep from getting busted? And what if something bad happened when they got there?" Joy wonders. "That dumbass sheriff will never figure it out."

Hope puts her hands over her ears.

"We should just go out together and see if we think it was Seth," Joy whispers. "Before Gaietto pins it on you, and I have to go alone."

Hope shakes her head and turns back into the couch cushion.

"We'll just go look around," Joy calmly directs.

Hope buries her face.

"We'll be in and out. Nobody will ever know we were there."

Hope takes a deep breath.

"Boys," Joy says, now loud enough for the kids to hear. "Go over to our house."

"I don't want to," Scott argues.

"Do it," Joy demands calmly. She scoops the puzzle back into the box. "You can take this with you."

Nicholas takes the box, takes his brother by the hand, and the two walk out the front door. Hope and Joy give it a minute, then head quickly out the same door, duck between the two houses, and walk toward their beat-to-shit Dodge Colt parked out back.

"I'll grab the keys," Joy says, stealthily mounting the back Murphy steps and steering into the kitchen without notice. She can hear Bridget talking to the boys.

Hope sees Bridget pass between the two houses.

Hope's car is not quite the same, but Mr. Murphy did a little magic with a wire hanger, so it's mobile. The twins leave, moving quietly past the Stimmells' barn and up Jackson St.

"I don't think Seth could take them both," Hope says. "They're both pretty badass."

"Right, but it's his old house, it's out in the country, there's nowhere for them to go," Joy says. "Maybe he saw them coming. Maybe he like hid behind the door and hit one of them in the head with a baseball bat or something."

Hope flinches.

"Dude, I'm all gimp, the car's all gimp," Hope realizes. "Maybe this is just a terrible idea because I don't see us getting away from danger. Not intact."

Joy ignores her.

"All those people who died in our neighborhood, too," Joy says. "He could have killed all of them."

"Not Brenda Cassidy," Hope says. "He didn't live here yet. He was probably, like, in high school."

Silence.

"Or Joannie Fabrizio—although she just disappeared, so maybe she's not dead."

"Maybe she's out at Seth's," Joy says.

"Seriously, though, we have no exit plan," Hope reminds her. "No exit plan, two infirm if you count the car. No way we make it out alive if he actually is the culprit."

"If Gaietto decides it's you, that's it. The end," Joy says, then she imitates him. "Don't you remember, folks? She wrote all about it in her school play. And who can forget how Satan had her writhing on the floor of the church, unable to make her Holy Confirmation?"

Hope sighs sadly, and they ride in silence.

"I already can't remember her voice," Hope whispers sadly. "I wish I'd paid attention to how she sounded before the ventilator. I just can't remember now."

Joy turns off the headlights and slows to a stop.

"We should have brought weapons," Hope says.

"We'll hide," Joy says. "See what's what."

The passenger door creaks loudly as Hope opens it, and the sisters freeze.

Joy gives Hope an accusatory eyeball.

"It actually wasn't my fault," Hope says. "A guy hit me."

"Uh-huh…" Joy says.

Hope stumbles over the dark earth between the road and field, but she finds her footing, and the sisters creep toward the old Oliver house.

There's a light on somewhere inside the house—they can see it through some of the windows as they get closer.

"Front door, back door, what?" Hope asks Joy.

"Try the front. It doesn't look like anybody's in that part of the house."

One following the other, they duck beneath a window and cut across the porch. Joy peers in through the screen door and sees nothing. She opens the door just far enough to squeeze through, and her sister follows.

The front room smells like dust and pot. Joy makes her way through the dark room with ease, but Hope stumbles over the clutter: a toolbox, a crate of albums, a stray shoe. An end table has been overturned, a broken lamp and ashtray spilled to the floor.

As they get closer to the lit back room—the kitchen, it turns out—they hear talking.

"Do you believe in redemption?"

That's what they hear.

The voice is not Seth's.

Hope slides up behind her sister, squinting over Joy's head to make out the second man, although she recognizes that voice.

Victor circles Seth. Seth's head swivels, following him around one side, catching him as he comes back around the other.

"Your young lover and a friend pound on your door late at night," Victor says. "They're out of breath. You're angry—you've just gotten off the phone with your ex-wife. She's been on a date."

Victor continues to circle.

"Your young lover suggests you get high, but her friend wants to use the phone. You'll show your wife, you think. What do you need with her when you can have two young girls?"

"You don't know anything," Seth whimpers.

"But your lover's friend isn't interested, is she? And when she tries to leave, you knock her down the basement stairs."

Seth stares in amazement and horror.

"It was an accident..." he offers.

"Of course, it was!" Victor agrees. "But the second girl, now that was deliberate."

"She'd have—"

"Screamed? Run? Brought justice?" Victor asks. "Can't have that. And why worry when the law is so easily led astray by a little garish Halloween scenery?"

Seth's eyes dart nervously around the kitchen. Victor walks close to him.

"Will you throw me down the stairs, too?"

Without ever looking Victor in the eye, Seth pushes him, but Victor doesn't budge. Seth's feet slip beneath him as if he's pushing a wall. He backs up, terrified.

"Your display, though!" Victor pantomimes a chef's kiss. "Inspired. Almost too creative for a weasel like you to come up with on your own, honestly. Most impressive. And your sheriff..."

Victor smiles wickedly, shakes his head.

"Well, he's perfect, isn't he? Every time a single mother's new boyfriend murders one of her kids, the least likely culprit—the special needs high school kid who listens to Ozzy Osbourne—gets the blame. Do you know what that does? That makes the town feel safe for every budding psychopath. Who needs an alibi as long as you drive a pickup, eat meat, and attend church?"

Victor takes a deep breath.

"Oh, I do love this town."

He turns his attention back to a red-faced, panicked Seth.

"Seth," Victor says, laying his hands on Seth's shoulders. Seth begins to cry. "Seth, I just want to know if you're sorry."

Seth looks Victor in the face. Seth is terrified.

"I…I…"

Victor lets go of Seth's shoulder.

"I…I…" Victor mocks him. "It's a simple enough question, Seth. Are you sorry?"

"I am."

"Sorry you've been found out," Victor clarifies. "But not sorry for what you did."

"I am," Seth promises. "I am sorry."

"If you had true remorse, you would pine for the recompense owed you."

"I shouldn't have hurt them," Seth cries.

"If you truly regretted your actions, you would cry out to make amends," Victor says. "Although amends cannot be made, can they? We can't even be certain that you wouldn't do it all over again, given the opportunity."

"I wouldn't," Seth promises, panic rising. "I would not."

"Can you be trusted to be alone with young, vulnerable women? Women just looking for a safe place to hide. Can you be sure you wouldn't lose control of yourself all over again? How did it feel, Seth? The give, the yielding, the blood? Did you feel powerful?"

"I would not ever—"

"But you won't cry out for your punishment, and you can't be trusted with the same situation because you are not sorry," Victor decides. "You can't be sorry because you are a coward."

Seth commands what he can of his courage and announces: "I am sorry, and I will be forgiven."

Victor laughs.

"Do you really believe this is forgivable?"

Pause.

"Let's be clear, then," Victor says. "It's not."

Seth begins to cry.

"Oh, Seth. Your only hope is that God doesn't exist. There is nothing for you to do but kill yourself," Victor reasons.

This shocks Seth from crying.

"What else is there?" Victor asks. "You're a sexual predator and a murderer. You'll go to prison, where you will no longer be the predator in a sexual situation. You'll have to face your sons and your wife and their shame. Honestly, what other option is there?"

"I can't," Seth says.

"Because?"

"Suicide is a sin."

Victor laughs loudly.

"Judas killed himself, didn't he? Did we mourn that? Or did we simply know, without sermon or clarification, that he had no other choice once he'd realized what he had done? Some things are unforgivable. If there is a God, Judas would live in misery and then go to hell. He simply ended the misery on earth. If no God, no hell, just release from misery."

"Don't you think that trying to talk someone into suicide might send a person to hell?" Seth asks accusingly.

Victor smiles broadly.

"I will most certainly join you on your journey."

"You're going to kill yourself?" Seth asks, confused.

"Of course not. I'm not a coward. And besides, I pose no threat to anyone," Victor pauses. "That matters."

Victor opens a drawer in a cabinet near a deep sink. He pushes aside a roll of duct tape, some loose pens, a box cutter. He produces a pistol.

Seth recoils.

"In the mouth, toward the top of the head, sure and painless," Victor advises. "Perfect for a coward."

Then Victor looks up, peering past Seth and into the darkness.

"Ladies."

Joy walks into the light.

Hope looks with horror at her sister, willing her back into the safe, comfortable shadows. Joy doesn't return, so Hope stumbles out to join her.

"We know what you're doing," Hope says.

She doesn't. She has absolutely no fucking idea what he's doing here, what's going on with these two, or what they're talking about. She grabs Joy's arm and tugs.

Victor circles them. They move further into the kitchen. Victor comes to a stop once he stands between the hallway to the front door and the sisters.

Hope searches for another way out.

"Nearly your birthday," Victor coos.

Hope decides on a window. How in the fuck is she going to get it open or broken, she wonders as she nudges Joy in that direction?

"It's a big one," Victor says. "Your birthday. Eighteen! On Easter Sunday."

Joy isn't moving. She's so small, though, Hope thinks. I can grab her and run—like a fireman's carry or something. Curse this gimpy leg! Her eyes move to a kitchen chair and a large window beyond where Seth stands.

"Help me," Seth mouths.

Hope winces. Fuck that guy.

"Easter isn't really a necessity," Victor says. "Just a bit of fun."

He smiles calmly, full of affection, and takes another step toward the sisters.

"Dude, back off," Hope says, standing closer to Joy.

"Hope," he says, patient but hurt. "You wound me. We have waited so long."

He takes Joy by the hand. She trades positions, standing next to him and looking at Hope.

Hope nearly follows her sister, drawn like a magnet, but she stops. Her lungs are empty, her stomach drops. Calmly, Joy waves her over. She holds her hand out, looks so peaceful.

He's looking at Joy, pleased and full of warmth.

He looks back at Hope.

"Don't keep us waiting any longer," he says. He looks affectionately toward Joy but doesn't touch her. She continues to look at Hope, nodding her head toward the empty spot next to her.

"What would you do without your sister?" he asks Hope. "Honestly."

He walks behind Joy, runs his hand over her hair.

"You'd probably be nothing but bones down the neighbor's basement, wouldn't you?"

Hope looks at her sister, raises her eyebrows.

"What the fuck," she seems to say. Joy looks back at her, disappointed.

Seth Oliver inches around them and toward the dark hallway that leads to the front door.

"What did happen to Joannie Fabrizio?" Victor asks with mock concern. He musses Joy's hair, says to her with a conspiratorial laugh, "Good thing Honey Gehrig never cleans out that basement, eh Joy?"

She smiles at him, and he chuckles to himself.

"What was that?" Hope wants to know.

"Hope," he says smoothly. "Don't you want to know what we did to Joannie Fabrizio?"

Hope's eyes dart toward Joy, who looks back at her calmly.

"Joy was so little," Victor remembers tenderly.

"Dude, this is nuts," she says to her sister.

"She sees things that you don't," Victor says. "Opportunities, truth."

"Yeah, she's a special little princess," Hope says snidely. "So, you're like a serial killer's apprentice?

Wait, wait. We didn't even know him then. This is not even—I don't even care. We just gotta go."

Hope grabs Joy's hand and yanks. Joy falls forward, and Hope pulls her toward Seth's hallway.

Victor puts an arm around Joy's waist.

"Dude," Hope says, struggling against tears. "Just stay where you are. We're just going to leave here and forget anything ever happened. Right? I mean, you know, whatever you two have been up to, well, I don't want anything to happen to Joy, right? So, no worries about us. Mum is the word."

Victor continues to smile. Joy pulls free of Hope, looking irritated toward her sister.

"Joy!" Hope yells. "Dude, let's move."

Victor's looking at Hope.

"You'll be a hero," Victor laughs.

She won't look at him. She stares pleadingly at her twin.

"He's a bad man, Hope," Victor continues. "A murderer with a predilection for underage lovers."

Joy shakes her head unhappily.

"A weaselly coward likely to take his frustrations out on delicate young women." He turns to Seth. "The way you used to take them out on your wife, right?"

Seth makes a break for it, but Victor reaches out, grabbing him as if they'd been standing inches apart.

Victor turns back to Hope.

"As the local authorities closed in on Oliver, he returned to the old farmhouse where he'd tried conjuring the devil, where he'd done unspeakable things with local girls," Victor states as if reading from a police report. "Realizing his days were numbered, he took his own life, but not before killing his wife."

"What?!" Hope blurts, startled.

Victor smiles, then holds the gun toward Hope.

"Then take care of it before she arrives," he says. "It is your turn."

Hope stumbles backward. Joy grabs her arm, steadies her.

Victor tilts his head, smiling patiently at Hope.

"We have waited so long," he says again.

Hope looks like she needs to sit down.

"You just have to do it this one time," Joy tells her. "And then we can get out of Odenton. Leave this fucking place."

Hope is nonresponsive.

Joy looks slightly desperate.

"You hate him, don't you?" Joy asks, pointing toward Seth.

"No," she says.

Seth sighs, relieved.

Joy and Victor look so disappointed.

"You have had so many opportunities, Hope," Victor prods. "Alone in that kitchen with Doug Young. Did you feel me there?"

He walks behind her, and she turns her head to follow, then looks back at her sister. Victor stands close behind her, whispers low.

"Did you feel me?"

He takes a step back.

"But those horrid would-be rapists in the laundry room?" he asks Hope with disappointment. "Or that ogre Cleofa!"

He laughs, looking over Hope's shoulder toward her sister. "Joy almost took care of that one for you, didn't you?"

He winks at Joy.

"The way she took care of Joannie Fabrizio for you."

He pauses. Walks back around Hope. Stands between her and her sister.

"For you," he says solemnly, drumming his fingers on the back of a kitchen chair. "Now, what are you going to do for us?"

Hope bends forward, loses her breath, steadies herself on the sticky kitchen table.

Victor holds the gun toward her, but she steps away from him.

"We have given you so many opportunities," he raises his voice. "You never take them. And so, your sister and I wait, year after year."

"Stop saying words," Hope says weakly.

Victor continues.

"Now, I'm hardly a stickler for justice, but that does not seem fair."

Hopes looks desperately at her sister.

"Dude, what the fuck?"

"Like he's doing anybody any good," Joy says flatly. "It's better for Regina. So much better for the boys. Think about that—he doesn't call their mom up and make her cry, doesn't hang around outside playing awful music and pretending to be tough while he's boning some high school girl. This makes sure he doesn't contaminate their lives."

Seth makes another move to leave, and Victor blocks him.

"How is it not a good thing?" Joy challenges.

"Did you kill Brenda Cassidy?" Hope asks suddenly.

"No." Victor responds for Joy. "No, that was her uncle, of course. And incompetent policework plus a town's distaste for the oddball."

"But you killed Joannie?"

"I require some proof. Some token, some sacrifice, some blood that ties my beloved to me."

"I gave you proof!" Seth shouts.

"You are not beloved," Victor calmly clarifies. "You took advantage of the heightened anxieties of the town to cover up your base proclivities. I had nothing to do with it. Though it is serendipitous if it moves our true beloved closer to us."

"The rules are arbitrary, really," Victor continues. "I like to challenge myself, make things fun. Eternity can be a bore. So long. An old woman dies on Easter Sunday as twin girls are born. It's the spectacle of superstitious idiocy and coincidence that arouses me."

He holds the gun toward Hope again.

"But, this sacrifice, it's honestly important. How else can I know that you are as committed to this relationship as I am?"

Hope looks at Joy, suddenly stricken.

"Isabel?" She is crying now.

"Oh, don't be like that," he says. "We were not responsible for your friend. Was I there? I mean, I was.

And when Katrina McCoy's brothers brought about her messy end in your neighbor's barn, and when the kid with nun-chucks returned to deposit his ex into the Coney Castle dumpster. But honestly, it's hard not to feel invited as much time and attention as this town devotes to me."

He pauses.

"Also, there's not a lot to do in Odenton."

"You couldn't have made him stop?"

Joy looks to Victor.

"Hope, my love. Our love. We think you loved Isabel better than you love your own twin sister. Now how is that for gratitude?"

"I didn't do it," Joy says.

Hope tries to capture her sister's attention, talk to each other as if this other person isn't really in the room, the way they have always done it. She fights the urge to flee.

"We need to just go," she whispers to Joy.

"Where would you go, Hope?" Victor asks.

"Can I just talk to Joy, please?"

She's crying. She wants to leave, wants Joy to snap out of it, wants Joy to knock Victor's legs out from under him while he's not looking so the two can run out the front door and toward the road where Joy can explain everything.

"That's not going to happen, Hope," Victor says gently. "Joy and I have been waiting for you for a long time. But you have to choose us."

She won't look at him. She stares at the floor, wills herself to stop crying, looks back up at Joy.

"It doesn't matter how you do it," Victor says. "Better if you don't bludgeon him to death with something, but if you want to stab him or even shoot him, believe me, they'll come up with some explanation."

"How do you even fucking know him?" Hope yells to Joy.

"We go way back," Victor laughs gently and takes a few graceful steps toward Hope.

Seth Oliver makes a break for it.

Victor holds the pistol out to Hope.

She recoils.

Joy takes it from Victor's hand.

Victor helps Joy aim it, steady it.

Seth rushes past a stack of TV trays in a dusty, gold-painted rack.

Victor lifts Joy's arm up slightly.

Hope holds her breath, stares at Seth.

"Now," Victor whispers, almost inaudibly, and Joy squeezes the trigger.

Hope gasps.

Seth goes down, yelping. He falls into the screen door, forcing it open, and lands awkwardly half inside, half outside the house. He drags himself forward, crying loudly.

Joy pushes the pistol toward her sister.

"Finish him," Joy says.

Hope does not take the gun.

"Oh my God," Hope says to her sister.

Joy shakes the gun at her sister impatiently.

"You have to do it," she says.

"She's right," Victor seconds Joy calmly. "We've waited a very long time, but it has to happen tonight."

"Fuck you."

"Just do it!" Joy yells. She grabs Hope by the arm and begins down the hall toward the screen porch door and Seth, who drags himself pitifully down the front porch steps crying. He's bleeding heavily from the bullet wound in his thigh.

"We've discussed this, Joy," Victor says.

"She'll do it," Joy tells him, then turns to her sister. "Do it."

"It would be a shame to separate you," Victor says.

"No," Joy says, just a touch of desperation breaking her voice. Then, to her sister, "Do it."

Headlights, the sound of car wheels on gravel.

Hope and Joy freeze. Victor looks on with curiosity.

The driver's door opens.

"Victor?"

It's Regina. Victor chuckles.

"Such a good soul."

"Regina! Run!" Hope yells.

"Help me!" Seth whimpers from the ground.

"Seth?!" Regina wonders.

In the darkness of the country, his body is hard to find on the ground.

"Regina, be careful—he has a gun!" Victor warns her.

Regina looks up, alarmed. She takes a few steps away from Seth, looking him over.

Victor vaults off the porch and moves toward Regina.

Regina has moved out of the light of her headlamps and toward Seth, crawling in the darkness.

"Regina!" Hope hollers.

She sees movement, but Regina is blocked by a larger figure moving in her direction. It seems enormous in the dark, vast and winged.

Hope grabs the gun from her sister and fires.

The figure vanishes, the darkness lifts, and Hope sees Regina's eyes widen as she drops to her knees and then to the ground.

"Nice shot," a seductive voice whispers in her ear.

"No, no, no, no, no!" Hope yells and stumbles off the front porch, dropping the weapon.

"She's not dead," Victor reassures her, bending to retrieve the tossed pistol. "She will be if we don't get her to town quickly to see someone who can sew that up, but we can't do that until you finish her husband."

"No!" Seth sobs. "Fuck you!"

"You'd let your lovely wife bleed out just so you can bargain for your own wicked life?" Victor accuses Seth.

"Please…" Seth begs, dragging himself slowly toward Regina's car.

Hope takes the gun from Victor's hand, marches toward Seth.

"No, no, no," Seth whimpers. He gathers his strength and yells, "Don't you fucking do it!"

Hope points the gun at Seth's head, pulls the trigger, and ends him.

Joy breathes deeply, relieved. Victor claps.

"So nice," he smiles, sliding next to Joy on the porch.

Hope sighs. She walks authoritatively toward the two on the front porch. She walks past Joy, approaches Victor, lifts the gun, and shoots him in the chest.

He falls.

Joy screams.

Hope turns to her sister.

"Let's get the fuck out of here," she says. She pulls her shirt away from her stomach to wipe the gun down.

"We'll get Regina. I'll drive her car; you drive ours. Don't leave anything here."

Joy isn't moving.

"Dude, snap out of it. We have to get Regina, get in her car, and leave."

Joy's staring past Hope to Victor, who's crumpled on the floor.

"Now, now, now!" Hope yells. "Did you leave anything anywhere?"

"Why did you do that?" Joy says quietly. "This town is shit. He would have looked after us."

Hope pauses.

"You look after us."

Joy looks at her sister, quietly surprised.

"I don't want to talk about any of this. Let's just get out of here, get Regina some help and let the adult men of the world come up with their own inaccurate story," Hope says. "We will Dodge Colt this bitch."

Joy's still staring past Hope.

"Dude, I will fucking carry you out of here," she says. Still staring past Hope, Joy smiles, and her eyes raise.

Hope stops breathing.

"I did not expect that."

Victor's voice is deeper, a growl. He lets out a breathy, sinister chuckle.

"Good for you," he says. "Not a lot of people surprise me."

Joy smiles again with relief. Hope stares straight ahead, frozen, terrified to turn around. Reflected in the front porch window, a form advances, tall and winged.

Hope closes her eyes.

"Believe it or don't, I am a forgiving sort," he whispers into her ear. "And difficult to kill."

Joy's smile spreads across her face. Standing close, directly behind Hope, Victor reaches a scarred arm past her face. Feathers flutter to the floor as he pats Joy's head, gently pushing away stray hairs.

"You fulfilled the requirement," he says. "And you surprised us."

He pauses.

"We will call that a bonus."

He circles Hope, takes Joy by the hand. Joy looks up at him lovingly. He looks like himself again.

"She was so worried that you wouldn't come along," he smiles, "and that we'd have to separate the two of you."

He looks tenderly at Joy.

"And after all her hard work looking after you! But now, the test is complete, and you are one of us. I know you will come to love us as we love you."

Victor turns Joy's face toward his. He leans in and kisses her.

Hope hears movement in the grass.

She feels the gun in her hand.

She lifts her hand and ends her sister's life.

Joy's body goes limp in Victor's embrace. He pauses momentarily. His face fills with rage. His body contorts, he grows enormous, wings rustle, and talons flash.

Hope ignores it. She stares at the blood flowing toward and pooling around her feet.

"Oh, Joy…"

She lifts the gun to her mouth.

"No!" Victor roars.

Hope blows the rear of her head across the muddy porch and drops in a heap, splashing Victor's boots with her sister's blood.

"Oh, Hope," Victor says, so quietly, so sadly. He sets Joy gently on the porch next to her twin. Completely transformed into the handsome, exotic outsider, he turns toward the sounds of struggle in the grass.

"Regina," he says weakly. "Regina, is that you?"

He walks toward her.

"You're alive," he says with joy. "I thought he'd killed all of you. Can you stand? I'll try to help you. We need to get to town, to a hospital."

"Hope and Joy," she says.

"They're gone," he says with genuine sadness.

"What?!" Regina asks, horrified.

"It was Seth," he says. "He shot them. He shot you. I don't know what all else he's done, but Hope killed him."

"What?" Regina asks, confused and quiet.

"She was very brave."

He helps Regina into the passenger seat of her still-running car.

"What will I tell the boys?" Regina asks, talking more to herself than to Victor.

Victor looks to the heavens. The moon is high in a black and empty landscape. It's nearly midnight.

"It will make for a tragic Easter," he says. "But things will be better by Christmas."

He pulls out, headlights throwing a glow on the wooden porch steps, blood trailing downward like ink tracing a story. Joy and Hope lie together, Hope's shirt soaking up Joy's blood, Joy's eyes open to heaven

Acknowledgements

I don't know whether to thank or apologize to my family, a clear source of inspiration for this book and so much else in my life. Thanks especially to Joy, who reads everything first and responds with measured and merciless wisdom.

My deep gratitude to Samantha Kolesnik for seeing something in this work and to Off Limits Press for giving it a home. Thanks, as well, to Waylon Jordan for his kindness and support during the editorial process.

Much appreciation and admiration go to artist Athena Kafantaris, whose sculpture inspired the cover image. And thank you so very much Claire L. Smith for the gorgeous cover art.

Thanks forever to Riley, my sweet boy and the greatest joy of my life. Most of all, thanks to George for endless support, inspiration and love. I love you.

Author Bio

Hope Madden is a writer, filmmaker and film critic based in Columbus, Ohio. Her poetry and short fiction have appeared in numerous journals including *Wild Goose Poetry Review*, as well as Z Publishing's *Best Emerging Poets: An Anthology.* Fueled by diet pop and horror shows.

CPSIA information can be obtained
at www.ICGtesting.com
Printed in the USA
LVHW030438220322
714056LV00010B/537